The Storyteller

Paul Klee, *Angelus Novus*, 1920

The Storyteller

Tales Out of Loneliness

Walter Benjamin

With Illustrations
by Paul Klee

Translated and Edited by
Sam Dolbear, Esther Leslie
and Sebastian Truskolaski

VERSO
London • New York

This edition first published by Verso 2023
First published by Verso 2016
Introduction and translation © Sam Dolbear, Esther Leslie
and Sebastian Truskolaski 2016, 2023
Translation of 'Nordic Sea' © Antonia Grousdanidou 2016, 2023
In Chapter 16, Albert Welti, *Mondnacht*, taken from
Albert Welti, *Gemälde und Radierungen*, Furche Verlag, Berlin, 1917
In Chapter 34, 'Wandkalender' © Akademie der Künste, Berlin,
Walter Benjamin Archiv
The images by Paul Klee are in the public domain

1 3 5 7 9 10 8 6 4 2

Verso
UK: 6 Meard Street, London W1F 0EG
US: 388 Atlantic Avenue, Brooklyn, NY 11217
versobooks.com

Verso is the imprint of New Left Books

ISBN-13: 978-1-80429-041-5 (PB)
ISBN-13: 978-1-78478-307-5 (US EBK)
ISBN-13: 978-1-78478-306-8 (UK EBK)

British Library Cataloguing in Publication Data
A catalogue record for this book is available from the British Library

The Library of Congress Cataloged the Previous Edition as Follows:

Names: Benjamin, Walter, 1892–1940, author. | Dolbear, Sam, translator,
  editor. | Leslie, Esther, 1964– translator, editor. | Truskolaski,
  Sebastian, translator, editor.
Title: The storyteller : tales out of loneliness / Walter Benjamin ;
  translated and with an introduction by Sam Dolbear, Esther Leslie and
  Sebastian Truskolaski.
Description: First [edition]. | Brooklyn, NY : Verso, 2016.
Identifiers: LCCN 2016013569 | ISBN 9781784783044 (paperback)
Subjects: LCSH: Benjamin, Walter, 1892–1940 – Translations into English. |
  BISAC: FICTION / Short Stories (single author).
Classification: LCC PT2603.E455 A2 2016 | DDC 833/.912 – dc23
LC record available at http://lccn.loc.gov/2016013569

Typeset in Caslon Pro by MJ&N Gavan, Truro, Cornwall
Printed in Great Britain by CPI (UK) Ltd, Croydon CR0 4YY

Contents

PART TWO: TRAVEL

City and Transit

Landscape and Seascape

PART THREE: PLAY AND PEDAGOGY

Walter Benjamin and the Magnetic Play of Words

Sam Dolbear, Esther Leslie
and Sebastian Truskolaski

Throughout his life, Walter Benjamin experimented with a variety of literary forms. Novellas and short stories, fables and parables as well as jokes, riddles and rhymes all sit alongside his well-known critical writings. He also long harboured plans to write crime fiction. There exists an extensive outline for a novel, to be titled *La Chasse aux mensonge*, detailing ten possible chapters, including such details as an accident in a lift shaft, an umbrella as clue, action in a cardboard-making factory, a man who hides his banknotes inside his books and loses them.[1] The sheer variety of Benjamin's literary texts reflects the often precarious existence that he forged as a freelance author, moving around the continent sporadically taking on assignments for newspapers and journals. The short forms collected in the present volume stand in their own right as works of experimental writing, but they also act as the sounding board for ideas that feed back into Benjamin's critical

---

1 See: Walter Benjamin, *Gesammelte Schriften VII, Nachträge*, ed. Rolf Tiedemann (Frankfurt: Suhrkamp Verlag), 846–8.

work. The Tsarist clerk Shuvalkin and the Hasidic beggar in 'Four Stories' (c. 1933–4), for example, resurface in his essay on Franz Kafka (1934).[2] Likewise, the Imperial panorama from 'The Second Self' (c. 1930–3) recalls the 'Tour of German Inflation' described in *One Way Street* (1928) as well as the essay on 'The Work of Art in the Age of Its Technological Reproducibility' (1934–5) and the autobiographical vignettes laid out in *Berlin Childhood around 1900* (1932–8).[3]

Charting these continuities is more than a mere exercise in philology. Rather, the purpose of bringing together these texts is to demonstrate how Benjamin formally stages, enacts and performs certain concerns that he develops elsewhere in a more academic register. Consistent across the work is an exploration of such themes as dream and fantasy, travel and estrangement, play and pedagogy. Before commenting directly on the specifics of this topology, however, a discussion of Benjamin's reflections on storytelling is warranted.

Benjamin treated the theme of storytelling in an array of texts, not least among them 'The Storyteller' (1936), an essay on the Russian novelist Nikolai Leskov from which the title of the present volume is drawn.[4] In another, a short text titled 'Experience and Poverty' (1933), Benjamin lays out the central

---

2   See: Walter Benjamin, 'Franz Kafka: On the Tenth Anniversary of His Death', in *Selected Writings 2.2, 1931–1934*, ed. Howard Eiland, Michael Jennings and Gary Smith (Cambridge, MA: Harvard University Press, 2006), 794–818.

3   Among other references see Walter Benjamin, 'One Way Street', in *Selected Writings 1, 1913–1926*, ed. Marcus Bullock and Michael Jennings (Cambridge, MA: Harvard University Press, 1996), 450–5; Walter Benjamin, 'The Work of Art in the Age of Its Technological Reproducibility', trans. Michael W. Jennings, *Grey Room* 39 (Spring 2010): 11–37; Walter Benjamin, *Berlin Childhood around 1900*, trans. Howard Eiland (Cambridge, MA: Harvard University Press, 2006), 42–4.

4   See: Walter Benjamin, 'The Storyteller: Observations on the Works of Nikolai Leskov', in *Selected Writings 3, 1935–1938*, ed. Howard Eiland and Michael W. Jennings (Cambridge, MA: Harvard University Press, 2006), 143–62.

claim he would later develop in the Leskov essay. Before the onset of the First World War, we are told, experience was passed down through the generations in the form of folklore and fairy tales.[5] To illustrate this claim, Benjamin relates a fable about a father who taught his sons the merits of hard work by fooling them into thinking that there was buried treasure in the vineyard by the house. The turning of soil in the vain search for gold results in the discovery of a real treasure: a wonderful crop of fruit. With the war came the severing of 'the red thread of experience' which had connected previous generations, as Benjamin puts it in 'Sketched into Mobile Dust'. The 'fragile human body' that emerged from the trenches was mute, unable to narrate the 'forcefield of destructive torrents and explosions'[6] that had engulfed it. Communicability was unsettled. It was as if the good and bountiful soil of the fable had become the sticky and destructive mud of the trenches, which would bear no fruit but only moulder as a graveyard. 'Where do you hear words from the dying that last and that pass from one generation to the next like a precious ring?' Benjamin asks.[7]

By contrast, the journalistic jargon of the newspaper is the highest expression of experiential poverty – a lesson that Benjamin learned from Karl Kraus.[8] As Benjamin comments, 'every morning brings us the news of the globe and yet we are poor in noteworthy stories.'[9] But it is precisely for this

---

5 See: Walter Benjamin, 'Experience and Poverty', in *Selected Writings 2.2, 1931–1934*, 731–5.

6 Ibid., 732. This wording is echoed almost verbatim in Benjamin, 'The Storyteller', 144.

7 Benjamin, 'Experience and Poverty', 731.

8 See: Walter Benjamin, 'Karl Kraus', in *Selected Writings 2.1, 1927–1930*, 433–58.

9 Benjamin, 'The Storyteller', 147. The irony that the newspaper is, for the most part, the forum in which Benjamin's literary efforts appear is not lost on him.

very reason that seemingly redundant narrative forms become highly charged. Benjamin's association of experience with folklore and fairy tales cannot be seen as expressing a nostalgic yearning to revive a ruined tradition. Rather, the obsolescence of these forms becomes the condition of their critical function – a point that Benjamin explores in the review 'Colonial Pedagogy' with reference to the attempted modernisation of fairy tales. Kafka's parables elude interpretation because the key to understanding them has been lost, yet the function of this anachronistic opacity is the unfolding of a language of gestures and names: a facet of what has been described as Kafka's 'inverse messianism'.[10] By the same token, it would appear that the moment for reading Baudelaire's lyric poetry had passed at the time of its publication, yet it is precisely the untimeliness of its presentation that imbues Baudelaire's rendition of modern life with the urgency that Benjamin admired. What Benjamin attempts to re-imagine in his engagement with these authors is the communicability of experience in spite of itself. In this regard, it is notable that a common trait of Benjamin's own fiction is the layering of voices in imitation of an ostensibly antiquated oral tradition: a sea captain tells a passenger a yarn, a friend tells another friend a curious thing that he experienced, a man tells the tale of an acquaintance to another man, who in turn relates the story to us. These stories create layered worlds of citations, enigmas and perspectives. With this, Benjamin extends a long tradition of recording and retelling stories which stretches from Hebel to Hoffmann and beyond. Here experience finds new ground.

Might it be said, then, that Benjamin is attempting to reactivate the orality of storytelling under new conditions? If so,

---

10 Sigrid Weigel, 'Zu Franz Kafka', in *Benjamin Handbuch, Leben – Werk – Wirkung*, ed. Burkhardt Lindner (Stuttgart/Weimar: Verlag J.B. Metzler, 2011), 543.

then what kinds of stories do the trenches demand? What writing speaks to the moment? What follows divides Benjamin's literary output into three sections: dreamworlds, travel, and play and pedagogy. Included are a number of reviews which address the themes in each section, focussing the material through a form that Benjamin pushes in extraordinary directions, to the point where it might undo itself.

The first section of the volume clusters around dreamworlds. Presented here are Benjamin's own transcribed dreams alongside some of his earliest writings. These early works of fantasy offer visions of a 'world without pain'[11] much as his night dreams mirror and exaggerate the pains of this world. The section on travel is divided into stories of transit through landscapes and seascapes, towns and cities. We see the lonely traveller and also the wanderer who gleans experiences from strange encounters in order to convey them back to an audience, just as in 'The Storyteller' the journeyman turned master conveys wisdom in the workshop.[12] Focussed here, too, are the erotic tensions of modern city life, a theme Benjamin explored since his earliest writings. The third section presents play and pedagogy as two intertwined aspects in Benjamin's thinking. Several pieces explore the play of words, as if – to invoke a phrase from Benjamin's review of Franz Hessel's *Secret Berlin* – 'words become magnets, which irresistibly attract other words'. To learn from and encourage children's delight at wordplay is axiomatic in Benjamin's thinking. In this section is a story titled 'The Lucky Hand', which features play in the guise of gambling. Is this a modern morality tale? Perhaps Benjamin wishes to convey lessons about instinct and intuition, about the sort of mimetic knowledge possessed by the body? Likewise,

---

11 Walter Benjamin, 'Imagination', in *Selected Writings 1, 1913–1926*, 281.
12 Benjamin, 'The Storyteller', 144.

'On the Minute' plays on the idea of learning how to interact with new technologies, specifically radio, another medium in which Benjamin honed his ability to engage audiences through oral presentation. The following pages briefly introduce each of these themes.

Dreamworlds

Benjamin's fragments of fantastical fiction number among his earliest writings: *Schiller and Goethe*, *In a Big Old City*, *The Pan of the Evening*, *The Hypochondriac in the Landscape* and *The Morning of the Empress* are all thought to have been written between 1906 and 1912.[13] At this point it was perhaps to literary writings that Benjamin principally aspired. In a 1913 letter to his friend Herbert Belmore, Benjamin explicitly describes *The Death of the Father* as a 'novella'.[14] A second 'novella' also written in the same year – reportedly on the theme of prostitution – appears to have been lost. Benjamin does not, however, use this term to describe any of his work again until 1929, in reference to 'Sketched into Mobile Dust'.[15]

Long dismissed as mere 'juvenilia',[16] these texts have received little scholarly attention to date. In tandem with his work for Weimar radio, which has been similarly marginalised for many years, Benjamin revived his efforts to write fiction over the course of the 1930s. During this period he produced numerous

---

13 See: Rolf Tiedemann's editorial remarks in Walter Benjamin, *Gesammelte Schriften VII*, 635.

14 Walter Benjamin, *The Correspondence of Walter Benjamin (1910–1940)*, ed. Gershom Scholem and Theodor W. Adorno, trans. Manfred R. Jacobson and Evelyn M. Jacobson (Chicago: University of Chicago Press, 1994), 31.

15 See: Benjamin, *Correspondence*, 189.

16 See: Tillman Rexroth's editorial remarks in Walter Benjamin, *Gesammelte Schriften IV, Kleine Prosa/Baudelaire Übertragungen* (Frankfurt: Suhrkamp Verlag, 1991), 1074.

short stories for newspapers and magazines, often out of 'tangible motives', as he admitted to Gershom Scholem.[17] (Several of the pieces collected here under the heading 'Travel', including 'Tales Out of Loneliness', stem from this period.[18]) Whatever may have caused the widespread disregard for Benjamin's early stories – they first appeared as an addendum to his *Gesammelte Schriften* in 1991 after having been omitted from a previous volume dedicated to his 'Kleine Prosa' – these pieces are of considerable interest for at least two reasons. For one thing, they distinctively employ certain narrative techniques that seldom appear elsewhere in Benjamin's work, for example, the uncharacteristic use of the second- and third-person form. More importantly, however, Benjamin's early stories anticipate a number of the theoretical concerns that he developed in subsequent years. Childhood and fantasy, in particular, come to the fore in his fairy tale–like prose.

If we acknowledge this confluence, then a number of Benjamin's works on fantasy come to bear directly on his stories. In 'A Glimpse into the World of Children's Books' (1926), for instance, Benjamin notes, 'Pure colour is the medium of fantasy, a home in the clouds for the playful child'.[19] This gnomic formulation is a condensed statement of ideas that first emerged around 1915–16: an emphatic notion of 'fantasy' (as opposed

---

17 Benjamin, *Correspondence*, 401 [translation altered].

18 As Tiedemann notes, a number of writings from this period – apparently itemised in an unpublished note – appear to have been lost. They include *Bettlergeschichte, Jenaer Geschichte, John–Heartfield-Geschichte, Das Erste Beste, Der Bettler als Käufer, Sevilla-Geschichte, Sotto Lefronde di Limone, Weinberggeschichte, Kapitalgeschichten* (*Der abgehängte Wagen, Der gewohnte Nachmittagsspaziergang, Das Testament auf dem Amtsgericht, Der denunzierte Bankier*), *Henkergeschichte, Nimbus, Anna Czyllac und der Astrolog, Weingeschichte, An der Mole, Die Fahrt der Heimdal* and *Warum es mit der Kunst, Geschichten zu erzählen, zu Ende geht.*

19 Walter Benjamin, 'A Glimpse into the World of Children's Books', *Selected Writings 1, 1913–1926*, 442.

to the purportedly limited Kantian 'imagination') that is yoked to 'pure colour'; a 'deforming' kind of perception associated with the formlessness of clouds, rainbows and the like; and a sense that 'all deformation of the world will imagine a world without pain'.[20] Goethe and Runge, Hoffmann and Scheerbart are never far away. Significantly, Benjamin associates these characteristics with childhood. As Eli Friedlander observes, 'The purely receptive, uncreative actuality of a paradisiacal order, of painless change and dissolution, of discrimination before judgement and concept, free from yearning and desire … is the prerogative of children.'[21] This sentiment is forcefully expressed in 'The Morning of the Empress', when Benjamin notes that it is 'the children' who seemed to understand the secret question of the sovereign, 'but she understood the language of the children, as little as that of thunder'.

One need not map out the far-reaching implications of this thought to observe that the suggestive force of Benjamin's considerations reflects back onto his stories.[22] They animate his portrayal of the 'small, eight-year-old girl' from 'In a Big Old City', whom he describes as 'gazing wide-eyed at the strange, colourful flowers … embroidered onto' her guardian's clothes. They determine his decisive use of colour in 'The Pan of the Evening', where dusk is said to weave 'a shining, pale ribbon of magic over the snowy mountains and low wooded hilltops'. They govern the recurrent theme of uncanny wanderings through dream-like vistas when, in 'Schiller and Goethe', Benjamin writes that 'shades of green and white – many

---

20   Benjamin, 'Imagination', 281.

21   Eli Friedlander, 'A Mood of Childhood in Benjamin', in *Philosophy's Moods: The Affective Grounds of Thinking*, ed. Hagi Kenaan and Ilit Ferber (Heidelberg: Springer Dodrecht, 2011), 47.

22   See: Heinz Brüggemann, *Walter Benjamin über Spiel, Farbe und Fantasie* (Würzburg: Konighausen und Neumann, 2006).

colours – glowed delicately within' a 'black mountain' upon which E.T.A Hoffmann is said to have 'shone from an undulating Baroque boulder'. This is to say nothing of the frequent meteorological metaphors. In 'The Hypochondriac in the Landscape', for example, 'storms and tempests' open Benjamin's account of a quasi-masochistic, fully automated sanatorium.

Presented also in this section is a dream diary. It does not represent, however, a dedicated and sustained attempt on Benjamin's part to record his dreams with as much fidelity as possible. The dream-notes left in the archive – collected together in Burkhardt Lindner's 2008 book, *Träume*,[23] from which these translations largely derive – are mainly dated from around the late 1920s into the 1930s. There is evidence to suggest that unlike Adorno, who wrote down his dreams upon waking with the intention of publishing them as a dream diary without commentary, making changes only in exceptional cases,[24] Benjamin elaborates upon content and omits detail ex post facto. The manuscripts are riddled with corrections and amendments, altered further for publication in newspapers and journals.

Elaboration and censorship of dreams is not surprising when one considers how many of Benjamin's friends, lovers, adversaries and acquaintances traverse his dreams. They include the playwright and short-story writer Carl Sternheim, the author and doctor Alfred Döblin, the painter Toet Blaupot ten Cate, the publisher Adrienne Monnier and the philologist Gustav

---

23   Walter Benjamin, *Träume*, ed. Burkhardt Lindner (Frankfurt: Suhrkamp Verlag, 2008). Many of the dreams that appear in Lindner's volume are taken from *One Way Street*, *Berlin Childhood* and *Berlin Chronicle*. However, the present collection focuses only on previously untranslated texts written in the first person.

24   See: Theodor W. Adorno, *Dream Notes*, trans. Rodney Livingstone (Cambridge: Polity, 2007).

Roethe. In relation to these figures, censorship is rife. In the typewritten manuscript of one of the dreams from 1933, the references to Benjamin's brother and to Döblin and the Stern-bergian circle have been crossed out in thick pencil.[25] In an earlier draft of the self-portraits, Jula Cohn appears as 'the lover' and then, under revision, simply as 'my girlfriend'. In another early draft, it is Nazis who first storm a café and not a 'mob', as in a later version.[26] In the last case it is clear that state censorship played its part, but the distortion of dreams should also be understood as psychic protection from the messages they carry.

When the energies of the night are wrenched into the day through the process of linguistic representation, repressed desires and wishes can no longer evaporate through a process of forgetting. Benjamin, in *One Way Street*, equates such writing-up with betrayal,[27] for it is in the moment of transcription that latent desires have to be confronted. Just as the person who wakes up after dreaming betrays the night with food, so too does the writer who reaches for a pen. Censorship operates to protect dreamers from their dreams. Elaboration operates to capture the intensity of the dream-experience against the inadequacies of memory and language. But censorship has a limit. To an audience familiar with Freud, records of dreams become stark declarations of desire, arguably more exposing than the speech-act conducted between the analysand and the analyst. Symbols are read as pathology and, in Benjamin's case, declaimed loudly in public.

The elaboration of dreams has never been a problem for interpretation or analysis, for it is in the telling and retelling, in the remembrance and mis-remembrance, that significance

---

25 Walter Benjamin Archive, Berlin, manuscript 1709.

26 Benjamin, *Träume*, 44; Benjamin, *Gesammelte Schriften IV*, 423.

27 Benjamin, *One Way Street*, 444.

might be drawn out. It is through this act that the latent content of the dream (its wishes and desires) might override the manifest content (its details and events). As Adorno famously surmised, it is in exaggeration that psychoanalysis finds truth[28] – and, to an extent, dreams are already exaggerations. Though dreams are universal, and their objects and images boundless in quantity and variation, in a formal sense they are fairly standard. When read as a literary form, they tend to disintegrate linear narratives. In this way, they represent a modernist aesthetic prior to the formal development of modernism, but this perhaps fails to fully encapsulate their significance. Everything that has been shattered under the conditions of modernity is shattered further by the dream and its transcription.

What persists through them is the suspension of natural laws: substances merge, physical laws are overridden, space is fractured, events occur without linearity, and nature – in one particular case – is absolutely reversed. Figures pass through walls, and lions do somersaults. In this sense dreams work against the hardening of law to provide images of redeemed (or, at least, another) nature.[29] But it should be noted that these tendencies are not unique to Benjamin's dreams. What is perhaps remarkable about the dreams here is how unremarkable they actually are. For, when written down as narratives, in their expression of desire outside physical, political and psychic constraints, dreams echo the general desire for a world that cannot so easily be imagined in the daytime. Benjamin's attachment to the Jungian image of the 'collective unconscious'

---

28 Theodor W. Adorno, *Minima Moralia: Reflections from Damaged Life*, trans. E.F.N. Jephcott (London: Verso, 2006), 29.

29 See: Walter Benjamin, 'Little History of Photography', in *Selected Writings 2.2, 1931–1934*, 510.

in 'Convolute K' of *The Arcades Project*, despite protestations of its proto-fascism,[30] can be understood as an acknowledgment of this tendency. Not only do dreams operate against the status quo, but they do so through a universal or collective impulse.

This is not to say that the dream sits outside nature or history; rather, the propensity to dream is both motivated and constrained by such conditions. In the opening of the short sketch 'Dream Kitsch' (1925), Benjamin writes that 'dreams have started wars, and wars, from the very earliest times, have determined the propriety and impropriety – indeed, the range – of dreams'.[31] Dreams shape history and are shaped by it. Dreamworlds are the displaced expressions of this world within a world of their own. It is imperative to read the dream historically, as that which breaks from the familial and from private neuroses. The content of dreams – if not sleep itself – no doubt transformed with each decade of the twentieth century, but Benjamin does not embrace the unbounded quality of the night-dream as a general and universal desire. Dreams are not simply open; they are desires conditioned, even 'determined' by history.[32] They thus hold to the anxieties, banalities and brutalities of each epoch as much as they point to the destruction of those conditions. Their world is our world as much as it is its inversion, and it is in this double movement that their use can be found and mobilised. The process of recording dreams might congeal an unformed block of memory and desire, thereby betraying it by casting its original images all too starkly in language. However, dreams still work against the conditions of the day – possibly to overwhelm them.

---

30   See: Theodor W. Adorno, 'Letter to Walter Benjamin, 02.08.1935', in *Aesthetics and Politics*, ed. Ronald Taylor (London: Verso, 1977), 113.

31   Walter Benjamin, 'Dream Kitsch', in *Selected Writings 2.1, 1927–1930*, 3.

32   Ibid.

Travel

Walter Benjamin professed a love of travel from early on. He claimed that it was stimulated by postcards from his grandmother, who undertook trepidatious adventures across land and sea. His imagination kindled by her postcards, he soon undertook dream-journeys to 'Tabarz, Brindisi, Madonna di Campiglio', sailing the world's oceans.[33] As he grew into an adult, he began to travel widely across Europe – to the far northern reaches of Scandinavia, to Moscow and Riga in the East, to Paris in the West – and he was drawn to the South, to Marseilles, Naples, Capri and Ibiza. The Mediterranean South figures on various occasions in his fictional writing. In this regard, he follows in the footsteps of the German Romantics, for whom Italy in particular was a source of fascination. In their accounts of travel to Italy, German writers often established a dichotomy between the realities of day-to-day life in their homeland and an idyllic South, an imagined elsewhere, which promised an escape from the cold conduct of German society. In the German psyche, North and South represent two irreconcilable poles.

Benjamin began to dislodge himself from Germany in 1917, seeking other homes – Bern, Capri, Moscow, Ibiza, Paris, Denmark. He went back to Germany during the late 1920s and early 1930s, working for the radio, for newspapers and writing reviews. But he sensed the changing times. With his precarious mode of employment as a freelance writer, he was always searching for the cheapest place to eat, sleep, read and write. He reports in his diary in 1931 that, having spent all of his money, he seriously considered living in a cave

---

33   Walter Benjamin, 'Berlin Chronicle', in *Selected Writings 2.2, 1931–1934*, 621.

on an island in the Mediterranean.[34] He observed that he would endure any deprivation not to have to return to Berlin. Benjamin was blown by historical forces from the cushioned bourgeois home of his childhood to the comfortless cave of the dispossessed.

The city's spaces, especially those that are perceived only in passing, unexpectedly, and made available to a particular gaze, provide material for stories. It is here that lives and locations intertwine, and someone with an ear to the ground might pick up on a thousand tragedies, misdemeanours, lost or fulfilled loves. The city absorbs history, reflecting and deflecting the markers of power. After wandering in Paris, one of the settings for these stories, Benjamin reports in his *Arcades Project*:

> There is the Place du Maroc in Belleville; that desolate heap of stones with its rows of tenements became for me, when I happened upon it one Sunday afternoon, not only a Moroccan desert but also, and at the same time, a monument of colonial imperialism; topographic vision intertwined with allegorical meaning in this square, yet not for an instant did it lose its place in the heart of Belleville.[35]

Belleville is perceived through a bifurcation of views: a topographical one, which sees the shapes of the land, its hills and depressions, or in this case its sand, which is evoked in the miserable stones and poor ugly housing; a historical one, which sees colonial imperialism, the snatching of Morocco by the French, Morocco's desolation and all that is implied in terms of political history and morality. Benjamin goes on:

---

34 See: Walter Benjamin, 'May–June 1931', in *Selected Writings 2.2, 1931–1934*, 471.

35 Walter Benjamin, *The Arcades Project*, trans. Howard Eiland and Kevin McLaughlin (Cambridge, MA: Harvard University Press, 1999), 518.

But to awaken such a view is something ordinarily reserved for intoxicants. And in such cases, in fact, street names are like intoxicating substances that make our perceptions more stratified and richer in space. One could call the energy by which they transport us into such a state their *vertu évocatrice*, their evocative power – but that is saying too little; for what is decisive here is not the association but the interpenetration of images.[36]

The street name is charged, a poetry available to all, a stratification and amplification of sense and senses that will cascade for those who are open to it, a cataract of connections, leading into and out of political, historical understanding and emotional truth. (The play on street names in 'Sketched into Mobile Dust' comes into focus here.) Benjamin draws out of the things he witnesses an interpenetration of images which is a concentration of the energies of the world in their most potent state, amplified because of the constriction of the space that holds them. The short story likewise focuses energies into a few pages, acts as a concentration of actual and possible realities. As in the diary form, these stories record something of a tangible, recognisable world, but also bring out the ways in which our encounters and our exposures are overwhelming, mysterious, at times magical and otherworldly.

To travel is to leave behind the familiar. It should be noted that the familiar has its secret side too, as Benjamin established in his review of Franz Hessel's novel *Secret Berlin*, which defamiliarises Berlin by casting it as 'the stage for an Alexandrine musical comedy'. Travel enables new rules and ways of life. In 'Voyage of *The Mascot*', the ship is a floating 'Magic City' where revelry is the norm and the captain holds no authority. But over time the revolutionary spirit of the ship morphs into

---

36   Ibid.

a monumental bureaucracy that clogs up action. In 'Detective Stories on Tour', a review essay, Benjamin details how the train carriage becomes a mythic space where various demons hold sway. The lonely traveller is exposed to a world in books that is not the usual one, and the rhythms of reading are realigned with the rhythms of the locomotive. Stations are thresholds to other worlds, as are harbours. Travel brings the threshold into view, as for instance in 'Nordic Sea' when Benjamin observes women who stand in the doorways of buildings to negotiate the 'strict boundaries of the house'. Thresholds between the world of rationality and hallucinatory realms are crossed in these stories, as for example in 'Sketched into Mobile Dust' when the traveller gains access to 'another realm – elevated, disenchanted and clarified at once', through an encounter with a graffitied early Gothic capital bearing the name of a demonic woman. The erotic yearnings kindled especially in the space of the city span Benjamin's writings. An early tale, 'Still Story', describes the journey home of a young female student pursued by the narrator, who stalks her to her door. The city itself becomes a threshold.

A number of these stories were written and set in Ibiza. Benjamin appears fascinated by the differences between peasant life and the lives of the metropolitan figures who find themselves there, usually as exiles from some previous existence. Such a person might misunderstand or misread the signs on the island, as does the narrator of 'The Wall', who is sent on a wild goose chase in pursuit of a place that does not exist, or rather he finds it back where he started, a place of misunderstanding. Travel leads somewhere and misleads, though in being misled, one also witnesses much that is not otherwise revealed.

Play and Pedagogy

When travelling from Ibiza to Paris in September 1933, Benjamin devised a number of riddles. This was a long-standing pursuit for him, his wife Dora and his brother Georg, who would exchange riddles on birthdays and at Christmas. Just as he collated the words and sayings of his son, Stefan, as he was growing up, so too did he glean insights from the way that children deploy language when confronted with a handful of words.[37] One example is 'Fantasy Sentences', constructed during Benjamin's stay in Moscow in the winter of 1926–7, which is probably based on the formulations of Asja Lacis's daughter, Daga. A similar experiment was disseminated to a wider audience in 1931, when Benjamin delivered a radio programme entitled 'Radio Games: Poets with Keywords'. Adapted from a Baroque parlour game, the programme presented listeners with a series of seemingly unrelated words with which they were to construct sentences. Though this programme has been lost to history, the listeners' contributions remain, having been published in the radio station's newspaper, the *Südwestdeutsche Rundfunk-Zeitschrift*.[38] The process of translation or transposition best reveals the mechanism at work here. The game is, in Benjamin's words, poetry by keyword. With each formulation, a horde of analogies open up. New constellations of meaning crystallise as every word – each with a multiplicity of meanings – enters into new relations with another. Here we find a pedagogy rooted in fantasy and the

---

37 Walter Benjamin, 'Opinions et Pensées: His Son's Words and Turns of Phrase', in *Walter Benjamin's Archive: Images, Texts, Signs*, ed. Ursula Marx, Gudrun Schwarz, Michael Schwarz and Erdmut Wizisla, trans. Esther Leslie (London: Verso, 2007), 109–49.

38 Walter Benjamin, 'Funkspiele Dichter nach Stichworten', in *Südwestdeutsche Runfunk-Zeitschrift* VIII/3 (1932), 5.

deformation of existing meanings, an interest that dates back to Benjamin's involvement with the prewar youth movement.

This conception of pedagogy cannot be disconnected from play. Play is at the centre of Benjamin's thinking. It appears in different guises. It is there as something peculiar to children. It is also something that the gods do with humankind, as indicated in this piece of marginalia that Benjamin wrote on a review in 1930: 'Collectors may be loony – though this in the sense of the French lunatique – according to the moods of the moon. They are playthings too, perhaps – but of a goddess – namely τύχη (Tyche, Goddess of Luck).'[39] Play is there in the concept of *Spielraum*, which Benjamin develops in his writings on the work of art in the age of its technical reproducibility: 'Technology aims at liberating human beings from drudgery, the individual suddenly sees his scope for play, his field of action [*Spielraum*], immeasurably expanded. He does not yet know his way around this space. But already he registers his demands on it.'[40] *Spielraum* – room for play or manoeuvre, a space in which some exploration may take place. In this instance, play is a result of technological change and exists in tandem with it, a reorganisation of the self in the world. This room for play is an imagined space, a potential for habitation and habituation contained in the technical form of film or radio. But play was also more universal for Benjamin. Play is what each child longs to do. Wherever the child exists, the likelihood is that a space of play will develop. The *Spielraum* conjures forth and expands imagination. It develops

---

39 See: Rolf Tiedemann and Hermann Schweppenhäuser's editorial remarks in Walter Benjamin, *Gesammelte Schriften I* (Frankfurt: Suhrkamp Verlag, 1974), 851.

40 Walter Benjamin, 'The Work of Art in the Age of Its Technological Reproducibility' (2nd version), in *'The Work of Art in the Age of Its Technological Reproducibility' and Other Writings on Media*, ed. Michael W. Jennings, Bridget Doherty and Thomas Levin, trans. Michael W. Jennings (Cambridge, MA: Harvard University Press, 2008), 45.

the capacity for motile thought, and it is manifest in the facility of children to let language slip. *Spielraum* develops through mishearings and misunderstandings. It prompts children's affection for the speculative space of fairy tales and silly stories.

But play is not something that resides in a world far from worldly affairs. Play involves toys, and toys emerge from the world of work, from particular webs of social relations, as Benjamin observed of the Russian toys that he saw in a Soviet museum during a 1926–7 visit.[41] These were made by craft labour, and they had found a safe asylum in the museum. The toys would not survive outside the museum's cabinets. The web of relations that formed them was dying. Though precious, they could not be works of art precisely because of their relation to the hand that made them and the hand that would play with them. In a note, Benjamin observes, 'Toy is hand tool – not artwork.'[42] That is to say, toys are tools for grasping the domain of the greater forms on which they base themselves. Handmade and manipulated by the hand as the child plays, they allow the child to pry a way into the cosmos of play and beyond that into the world itself.

Play is also present where Benjamin imagines strategies for revolutionary overhaul. His 1928 review essay 'Toys and Play' considers the repetitive aspect of children's playful engagements.[43] The essay reflects on the ways in which children play, a topic which, according to him, has fallen by the wayside. He argues further that children's play proposes a mode of thinking that extends beyond itself, much like folk art, another 'primitivist' form that has the character of a model: 'Folk art and

41 See: Walter Benjamin, 'Russian Toys', in *Walter Benjamin's Archive: Images, Texts, Signs*, 107.

42 Ibid., 73.

43 See: Walter Benjamin, 'Toys and Play', *Selected Writings 2.1, 1927–1930*, 117–21.

the worldview of the child demanded to be seen as collectivist ways of thinking.'[44] Children take on the form of the new collective. Collectivist modes of thinking will, according to Benjamin, find historical shape in the Russian Revolution. In post-revolutionary Moscow he saw how 'the liberated pride of the proletariat is matched by the emancipated bearing of the children'.[45] The Bolsheviks conjoined the action of collective emancipation – or at least its outward sign – and the lives of children. In 'Programme for a Proletarian Children's Theatre' (1929), Benjamin observes: 'Just as the first action of the Bolsheviks was to hoist the Red flag, so their first instinct was to organize the children.'[46]

Where there are children, then there is also the work of learning. Benjamin did not disassociate play from pedagogy, and pedagogy was something that he returned to in various reviews and writings, beginning with his first published piece in 1912. This was a scathing critique of Lily Braun's *The Emancipation of Children: A Speech to School Youth*.[47] As Benjamin writes, the 'new youth, who out of the consciousness of themselves as *youthful people* place once more a higher sense and purpose in their existence',[48] render today's schools as ruins. Theirs is a revolution in consciousness, in modes of apperception and apprehension – a point that anticipates his subsequent work on fantasy. As he matures, Benjamin builds on his early insight that play and playfulness facilitate learning, a communist learning, perhaps, that unlearns bourgeois morality

44   Ibid., 118.

45   Walter Benjamin, 'Moscow', in *Selected Writings 2.1, 1927–1930*, 27.

46   Walter Benjamin, 'Program for a Proletarian Children's Theatre', in *Selected Writings 2.1, 1927–1930*, 202.

47   See: Walter Benjamin, 'Lily Braun's Manifest an die Deutsche Schuljugend', in *Gesammelte Schriften III*, ed. Hella Tiedemann-Bartels (Frankfurt: Suhrkamp Verlag, 1972).

48   Ibid., 11.

and undermines the training for war and death. For example, Benjamin's 'Four Tales' draw on the folk wisdom expressed in parables from the past, whilst also echoing aspects of Brecht's work, where the anecdotal form is used as a modern learning model. Morality is undone by a politics of modernism.

Benjamin undertook his own experiments in pedagogy, broadcasting regularly on German radio to the children and youth on topics such as liquor bootleggers, Berlin dialects, the petrification of Pompeii, counterfeit stamps, slum housing, manufacture, the legend of Caspar Hauser, the history of the Bastille prison, witch trials and the history of toys. Benjamin spoke about the history and curiosities of Berlin, about figures from the shadow side of life and about catastrophes. Through these broadcasts, as well as radio plays and playful programmes that set riddles or puzzles, he drew the children of Berlin and Frankfurt into modes of thinking, perceiving, drawing connections and counteracting the conventional history of their cities, their dialect and their homes, revealing cities within the city and illuminating their forms.

The German word for play or game is *Spiel*. This same word relates to gambling. *Der Spieler* is a gambler. The activity of gambling and the figure of the gambler appear at various points in Benjamin's work. Gambling is a decayed form of divination. In his file on 'Prostitution, Gambling' in *The Arcades Project*, Benjamin wonders about the links between the two: 'Were fortune-telling cards around earlier than playing cards? Does the card game represent a deterioration of soothsaying technique? Perceiving the future is surely decisive in card games, too.'[49] In his first sketch for *The Arcades Project*, Benjamin draws a link between automata and gods.

---

49 Benjamin, *The Arcades Project*, 514 [translation altered].

In front of the doorway to the ice rink, the local pub at those day-trip resorts, the tennis court: penates. Guarding the threshold: The hen who lays the praline-eggs of gold, the vending machine that punches out our names, machines for games of chance, the automated fortune teller. Strangely enough, such machines do not flourish in the town, but are more likely to be found as something at places where day trips happen, such as beer gardens in the outskirts. And, on a Sunday afternoon, out and about on the hunt for a little greenery, one is also heading to enigmatic thresholds. P.S.: coin-operated automatic scales – today's *gnothi seauton* (Know Thyself).[50]

In the game, a sporty one perhaps, in the act of gambling, placing the ball in the roulette wheel or laying the card, in divination by cards, entrails or stars, each player is aware of what move to make only at a subliminal bodily level. They mobilise, if they are to be successful, a motor reflex that works below the workings of the conscious mind. This appears as fate and is a communion between body and the order of the world that is present in the story 'The Lucky Hand' and that Benjamin returns to again and again. But such a version of things does not send play completely into a mystical realm. And indeed the gambler may misjudge, may make a wrong move, a false play. As Benjamin states, 'The ideal of the experience formed by shock is the catastrophe. In gambling this becomes very explicit; by persistently raising the stakes, in the hope of retrieving what is lost, the gambler steers toward total ruin.'[51] For Benjamin, gambling, as well as fate, has its historical materialist side. One of the striking aspects of nineteenth-century capitalism, as represented in *The Arcades Project*, is its simultaneous naturalisation and mythologisation of social and historical forces as fate. This

---

50   Ibid., 855–6 [translation altered].
51   Ibid., 515 [translation altered].

took on various forms, such as the language of a seemingly self-propellant rising and tumbling of stocks and shares – a consequence of the misconception (or ignorance) of the value-form, of playing the market, of prophecies of wide-scale destruction. Benjamin quotes from Paul Lafargue's 'The Causes of Belief in God' (1906):

> Today's economic progress in general inclines ever more to transmute capitalist society into a colossal international gambling house, where the bourgeois wins and loses capital as a consequence of events which remain unknown to him ... The 'inscrutable' is deified in bourgeois society just as it is in a gambling venue ... Triumphs and losses, which are the result of causes that are unexpected, in the main indecipherable, and apparently reliant on chance, predispose the bourgeois to adopt the spiritual condition of the gambler ... The capitalist, whose prosperity is bound up with stocks and shares, which are dependent on deviations in market value and yield whose causes he does not understand, is a professional gambler. The gambler, nonetheless ... is a highly superstitious type. The habitués of gambling hells always possess magic spells to conjure up the Fates. One will mumble a prayer to Saint Anthony of Padua or some other spirit from the heavens; another will lay his bet only if a specific colour has won; while a third clasps a rabbit's foot in his left hand; and so on. The inscrutable in society shrouds the bourgeois, just as the inscrutable in nature the savage.[52]

Play and playing, toys and mimicry: these crack open the world. But the impulse of play leads back to the dreamworld, to wishing and longing, to the gambler's yearning to make the greatest win, and it leads back to the desires that both mitigate and make blind to the catastrophe of economic rule. In

---

52 Ibid., 497 [translation altered].

'Verdant Elements', Benjamin celebrates the attitude of 'exaggerated exuberance' in a children's learning primer written by Tom Seidmann-Freud. Such an attitude informs all of Benjamin's works of fiction, be it the wild excesses of the early night-dreams and fantasies, the tall tales of wanderers and adventurers and the absurd reasoning in origin myths and riddles. Benjamin wrote the following of the consummate storyteller Proust: 'He lay on his bed racked with homesickness, homesick for the world, distorted in the state of similarity, a world in which the true surrealist face of existence breaks through.'[53] The same can perhaps be said of him and his own fictions.

---

53   Walter Benjamin, 'On the Image of Proust', in *Selected Writings II, 1927–1934*, 240.

PART ONE
Dreamworlds

Fantasy

CHAPTER I

Schiller and Goethe
A Layman's Vision

The sky had spread out a select German summer night between the trees. But as during a rococo rendezvous, the moon emitted a discreet yet bright yellow. Curling blossoms trembled down from the trees into the dark moss like yellow strips of confetti. The gigantic outlines of the great literature pyramid towered in the blue darkness. It was cosily uncanny. And now it lay there. Its peak stood out against the clear sky. Shades of green and white – many colours – glowed delicately within the black mountain. E.T.A. Hoffmann shone from an undulating Baroque boulder that protruded half toppled from the mound. The moon illuminated him. At the bottom yawned a black gate. In the uncontrollable twilight, its pillars appeared like Doric columns, *Iliad* on the one, *Odyssey* on the other. A white marble staircase glowed halfway up the pyramid. Upon it moved, quick as a monkey, the silhouette of a thin little man who continually called out 'Gottsched, Gottsched' in an unspeakably bright voice ... so quiet was his call that it was only audible in this fairy tale silence. In the dark depths, as though from an abyss, protruded a desolate heap of rocks. Slopes tore it apart, dirt and snow lay in its crevasses. A harsh wind howled from it. Shadows of kings, sad women, and on a small green patch of grass before a cave, beautiful mist-elves sat in a circle and laughed at a strange lion with baggy fur that roared like a human. I turned around. I felt dreadful that night. I proceeded to the hill of the wise owls. I spun round in a circle three times until I sprayed fire and called out, 'Wisest owl, *Eulenberg, Eulenberg*, wisest owl, wisest *Eulenberg*.' At first it was totally still, then there was a rustling in the trees. Then I heard a thin, sharp voice calling out from above. 'Wait!' A man with a walking stick came down the mountain. The night owls shrieked and fluttered as he advanced. He was wearing a brown frock coat and a beautiful, albeit slightly dented top hat. We did not exchange a single word. He walked ahead. Initially our ascent was quite comfortable. Broad marble steps led us past chasms from which ruined temples jutted forth, echoing with the sad rush of mighty rivers. A portly gentleman sat on a bench by the parapet. Snugly, and with a sour smile, he rubbed his hands. He had a wax tablet and a stylus in front of him. As soon as he saw us, he began to write slowly. 'Horace – the first man of letters', noted my guide in a sharp tone of voice. Suddenly I was brought up short. On a ledge I saw a man in a heavily wrinkled toga. One could see that he spoke continuously, his weak body quivering from exhaustion. He appeared to be yelling and yet one could hear no sound. All around him was empty. Terror seized hold of me. 'Cicero', whispered my guide. The comfortable steps came to an end. Stony, unruly paths appeared in their stead. The boulders took on strange shapes: slender stone flowers blossomed forth from them. Lining the way were rubble heaps, in front of which stood walls with tall pointed windows. Occasionally an organ sound seemed to become faintly audible. After some time we came upon a road in open country. A tiny little man with a greyish-green hood over his head fled as we approached. Quickly my guide took off his top hat. He wanted to trap the little fellow but he got away. 'Opitz', my guide remarked regretfully. 'I would have liked to have had him for my collection.' Then we walked for a long time along the dull country road. Suddenly a mountain appeared ahead of us. Upon it we saw, set against the sky, the silhouette of a writing man. He had an enormous sheet before him, and his pen was so long that it seemed to write in the heavens when he moved it. 'Take off your hat', I heard the voice beside me say, 'that is Lessing'. We greeted him, but the mighty figure on the peak did not move. There were dense shrubs at the foot of the mountain. The trees were finely trimmed. Little people moved around on paths like automatic puppets dressed as shepherds and beaus. Many danced around white statues that stood amid the greenery. A faint chirping rang from this party of puppets in the moonlight. But occasionally it was silent and a mighty voice riven with woe and longing and joy could be heard penetrating as far as the stars. 'Can you hear Klopstock?' I heard my guide ask. I nodded. 'We will be there soon,' he announced.

We went around the mountain and before us lay another dark plain from which two bright temple-like structures arose. With horror I noted that the immense chasm opened up beside us, with its temple ruins and roaring streams. Along its side swayed a figure, inching closer and closer towards the edge until – finally – it plunged before our eyes. 'Yes, we have arrived,' remarked my guide. 'Did you see Hölderlin?' Once again, I nodded silently and in terrible fear. The clear air was filled with strange cries. The deep yet beautifully constant tone of the sad streams reverberated from below. The sunken man's bright, woeful song seemed to mingle with it. From behind our backs resounded Klopstock's booming song. But the closer we drew to the two tall structures, the lighter it got and the sound began to fade. One structure towered above a tall, irregular boulder: it stood alone. Many people surrounded the other one. Men with large flags and kettledrums and others with feathers and bows sat around it. Screams came from the crowd. A great many lecterns stood all over the place, from which wildly gesticulating people preached. Some bellowed loudly up to the temple, 'Our Schiller!', but nobody came. Here my guide turned a corner. Soon we stood before the solitary temple. Hastily, a wizened little man in a tightly buttoned frock coat came hopping down the tall, broad stairs. 'Haha, our Eckermann', he giggled. An authoritative and unfriendly glance from my guide made him wince. He led us upwards.

I felt a quiet tremor in the stone structure under our feet. To my surprise, I simultaneously heard a sound like a distant drone. The farther we climbed up the tall marble steps, the more fiercely the ground shuddered, and the louder the drone echoed. It did not leave us again. As we entered, a dense darkness enveloped us. The mighty noises, which seemed to come not only from the ground but equally from either side of us, shook me. At the same time, I felt a transformation within myself. All my senses seemed to draw new strength from a force located within, which heightened them two- and tenfold. In the dense darkness, I could see; I felt with my eyes. I could feel myself in a large empty room. On every side, there were doors, gates and passages of every conceivable shape and size. Nearest to me was a bulky round doorway. It was tightly boarded up with wooden planks, between which protruded thick iron rods. From inside sounded the muffled ringing of ferocious bells. Further along, an equally wide Gothic gate swung open. Behind it, in the twilight, there appeared to be a room. Bright laughter came from the corridors that led inside. From time to time the figure of a biblical prophet appeared in the strange light; people in brown tails carrying feathers and bows hurried around the room and a young man spoke in a deep, sonorous voice: 'To be or not to be.' Aside from that it was silent amid the lively commotion. Magnetic forces seemed to inhabit the depths of the temple. It became hard for us to walk. Ahead of us lay a range of portals – some larger, some smaller – all in a heavy, gold-flourished Baroque or Empire style. They were closed, but from behind them – perceptible amid the subterranean storm – came fine music. And opposite, at a great distance, an open, illuminated room became visible, from which a wealth of marble statues emitted their glow.

Beside us stood Mephisto. He trod on ahead up some steep, narrow stairs – it may have been a thousand steps. We stood on one of the temple's elevated platforms. A wide, clear view of the earth spread out before us and we drank it in. But soon a stirring became discernible in this smooth, calm scene. It swelled and grew. The land appeared to surge in great waves. The sky darkened and contracted. It was as if the entire world drew together into this one point with terrifying force. While fleeing, we caught sight of torn laurel leaves strewn on the ground. Behind us resounded Mephisto's bright laughter. We reached a narrow corridor that continued on for an inestimable distance. Suddenly Mephisto's voice was with us again. Clearly and scornfully, but in a low voice, he seemed to ask a question: 'To the mothers?'

—

Translated by Sebastian Truskolaski.

Fragment written c. 1906–12; unpublished in Benjamin's life-time. *Gesammelte Schriften VII*, 636–9.

Opening part image: *Woman and Beast (Weib und Tier)*, 1904.
Opening chapter image: *The Balloon (Der Luftballon)*, 1926.

CHAPTER 2

In a Big Old City
Novella Fragment

There once lived a merchant in a big, old city. His house stood in one of the very oldest parts of town, on a narrow, dirty little alley. And on this alley – where all the houses were so old that they could no longer stand alone and had to lean against each other – the merchant's house was the oldest. But it was also the biggest. With its mighty, arched doorway and tall, curved windows made up of half-blind bullseye panes, and with the steep roof on which a number of narrow little skylights had been fitted, it looked quite strange – the house of the merchant, the last house on Mariengasse. This was a pious town and many of the houses had beautiful carvings of the holy virgin or some other saint above their doorways or under their roofs. On Mariengasse, too, every house had its saint – only the merchant's house stood bare and grey without any adornments. Nobody lived in the big house except for the merchant and a small eight-year-old girl. The girl was not his daughter, but she lived with him; he brought her up and the child helped with the housekeeping. But how she came to live in the merchant's house, nobody really knew. The merchant was not some ordinary grocer from whom the people bought clothes or spices – no! Nor did he keep company with the poor, common residents of his street. Day in and day out, he sat in his large study with the tall cabinets and long shelves and did his accounts and calculations. For his trade extended far across the seas to far-flung, distant lands. At intervals – perhaps once or twice per year – he had to leave his house for an extended period, when his business affairs summoned him far away. At these times, the girl stayed home by herself and took care of the household. One day the merchant-lord stood, once again, before the girl to tell her that he was leaving home for some time. 'I don't know when I will return,' he said. 'Take care of the house as you have before – *but*', he interrupted himself, 'I see you are old enough now; during my absence you can do as you please in the house. Here, take the keys.' The girl, who up until this point had stood silently in front of him, gazing wide-eyed at the strange, colourful flowers that were embroidered onto the lord-merchant's clothes, looked up and took the keys. Suddenly the merchant-lord looked at her with intent. Then he spoke in a stern tone of voice: 'You know very well that you may use the keys only for the rooms in which you see to the household chores. Never let yourself be tempted to ascend to the upper floor. Do you understand?' Timidly the girl assented. Then the merchant bowed down, kissed her, looked at her once more with a penetrating gaze, went down the stairs and left the house. The front door slammed shut behind him with a bang. The girl was still standing by the stairs in a daze, gazing at the large bundle of ancient keys that she held in her hand.

—

Translated by Sebastian Truskolaski.

Fragment written c. 1906–12; unpublished in Benjamin's lifetime. *Gesammelte Schriften VII*, 635–6.

Opening chapter image: *Two Facades (Dwie fasady)*, 1911.

CHAPTER 3

The Hypochondriac in the Landscape

ONLY FOR GROWN-UPS. NERVOUS TYPES – BEWARE!

Above the landscape hung such storm clouds as cause that specific fear of storms among young people known to physicians under a Latin name. It was a gently apprehensive mountain scenery. The path was steep and tiresome; the air was very hot and high temperatures prevailed. A mature man

– greyed by the passing of the years – and an adolescent moved as inaudible points through the silence. They carried an empty stretcher. From time to time the gaze of the younger man fell upon the stretcher and his eyes would fill with tears. It was not long before a doleful song streamed forth from his mouth, reverberating from the mountain with a thousand sobs. 'Red of the morning, red of the morning lights the path to an early death.'[1] In the distance, bloody bolts of lightning tinged the sky. Suddenly the singing broke off and was followed by a faint groan. 'Permit me for a moment', the young man said to the elder one. He rested the stretcher on the ground, sat down, closed his eyes and folded his hands.

At the peak of the landscape we find him again. A ruin stood there, overgrown by the green of nature. Storms and tempests roared more fiercely here than elsewhere. The place was created for the indulgence of every conceivable suffering … Special weight was placed on melancholy, which took place between seven and eight o'clock each evening. A valley located in the shadow of the sinking sun turned out to be suitable. Moreover, a box of eyeglasses with black and dark-brown lenses was on hand, which could enhance the melancholia to a state of horror and raise the evening temperature from 37° to a feverish 40°. When the moon was full, 40° was the minimum temperature and a flag was raised to signal mortal danger.

The beautiful summer nights were used for sleeplessness. Nevertheless, the patients were awoken as early as five a.m. for their morning diagnosis. Monday and Friday mornings were devoted to testing for anxiety; Sundays were for nightly indigestion. Thereafter ensued six hours of psychoanalysis. Subsequently hydrotherapy, which was administered

---

1   'Morgenrot, Morgenrot, leuchtest mir zum frühen Tod.'

telepathically due to the water, which tended to be wet and cold throughout most of the year. There followed a break at noon. It was dedicated to telephone consultations with European luminaries and to the theoretical exploration of diseases that have hitherto remained untargeted.

The meals are served in a chemically cleansed *Bazillopher*,[2] surrounded by ether and camphor fumes. The physicians oversee the procedure with a loaded rifle in order to slay any attacking germs. After being checked for various pathogens, the germs are doused with hot water, anatomically dissected, and killed. They then either appear on the supper table or in the exhibition rooms of the library, which contains the directory, description, danger and cure for all the diseases weathered by the patients to date.

For the twenty-fifth anniversary of each disease, a splendid monograph with cinematographic images is published. The library is open to patients between four and five every day and serves, above all, to incite new illnesses.

After dinner, physicians and patients organise germ hunts in the park. Oftentimes it happens that a patient is accidentally shot. In such cases a simple bed of moss and forest herbs is prepared as the patient sinks to the ground. Bandages lie ready in the tree hollows.

Everything has been provided for. Should the physician fall ill, an automatic operating room is provided, whose automated apparatuses perform all procedures upon the insertion of three to twenty pennies. At three pennies, the cheapest operation entails the chemical cleaning of the nose; for twenty pennies one can get treatments with life-threatening consequences.

---

2   A neologism coined by Benjamin which plays on the word *Bazille*, meaning 'germ' or 'bacteria'.

One evening, a serious tête-à-tête took place. The following morning, the physician disappeared on a clinical study tour to explore the latest diseases.

—

Translated by Sebastian Truskolaski.

Fragment written c. 1906–12; unpublished in Benjamin's lifetime. *Gesammelte Schriften VII*, 641–2.

Opening chapter image: *Aged Phoenix (Invention 9) (Greiser Phönix [Invention 9])*, 1905.

CHAPTER 4

The Morning of the Empress

Healthy people must turn to the books of poets in order to feel life in all the deep and undivided sovereignty that cannot be grasped intentionally, to feel it as it was felt by that ailing Empress of Mexico on the third day of spring in the year 18–. She had been brought to this palace such a long time ago that no one could keep track any longer. Who even thought that she was ill? None of her maids and servants – all of whom led boring lives inside this palace, only rarely tending to excess – believed it. A person had arrived whose beautiful, ageing body required all the care that servants could offer. She was loved by all for her splendour. The farmers from the environs of Palace

Drux told tales of this Empress who was foreign to the land, who was only supposed to die in that broad palace which towered above the plains of Holland.

But the Empress did not think of death, nor did she feel the life that stirred around her; accordingly she could be called disturbed of mind. Each evening when the sun went down, she pursued anew the question that haunted her like one of the broad paths that transforms in the twilight. This question was secret, and although the Empress had disclosed it to people she interacted with, the only answers she received were evasive, uncomprehending excuses – almost enough to infuriate – so that the Empress descended further and further down the ranks with this question: from the lady's companion to the chamber maid, from the maid to the equerry, from the equerry to the cook, and – finally – to the children. And, indeed, the children seemed to understand her question; but she understood the language of the children as little as that of thunder, although she had often begged this of God while kneeling on a prayer stool by the window. A vault lay in the basement of the palace, dark and filled with bottles of wine – there the Empress had struggled most deeply with the question. Hunched over, her tall figure under the low ceiling, she had fashioned a set of scales out of yarn and little tin bowls. She deemed these scales to be fine enough to examine the weight of the world. And this was her question.

———

Translated by Sebastian Truskolaski.

Fragment written c. 1906–12; unpublished in Benjamin's lifetime. *Gesammelte Schriften VII*, 642–3.

Opening chapter image: *The Witch with the Comb (Die Hexe mit dem Kamm)*, 1922.

CHAPTER 5
The Pan of the Evening

The evening had woven a shining pale yellow ribbon of magic over the snowy mountains and low wooded hill-tops. And the snow on the peaks shone pale yellow. The forest, however, already lay in darkness. The glowing of the peaks awoke a man who sat on a bench in the forest. He looked up and relished the strange light from the peaks, looking into it until he had only a radiant flickering in his eyes; he thought nothing more and only saw. Then he turned to the bench and took the walking-stick that leaned there. He said to himself, reluctantly, that he had to return to the hotel for dinner. And he trod slowly on the broad path leading down to the valley, watching his step because it was dusk and there were roots protruding from the ground. He did not know why he walked so slowly. 'You look ridiculous and pathetic stalking along on this broad path.' He heard these words clearly and with some indignation. He stopped defiantly and looked up at the snowy mountain tops. Now they too were dark. As he observed this, he clearly heard a voice inside him, a completely different one, which said 'alone with me'. For this was its greeting to the darkness. Hereupon he lowered his head and trod onwards against his will. He felt as though he was about to hear another voice which was mute and grappled for speech. But that was despicable ... The valley was in sight ... The lights from the hotel were surging up. As he peered into the grey depths below, he fancied he saw a workshop down there. He felt from a pressure on his own body how giant hands were forming masses of fog, how a tower, a cathedral of twilight arose. 'The cathedral – you yourself are within it,' he heard a voice say. And he looked around as he walked on. But what he saw seemed to him so marvellous, so stupendous ... yes (quietly he felt it: so terrible) that he came to a stop. He saw how the fog hung between the trees, he heard the slow flight of a bird. Only the nearest trees still stood there. Where he had just been walking, something else had begun to spread, something grey. It covered up his steps as though they had never been taken. He realised as he walked here that something else walked through the forest too; a spell presided over things that made the old disappear, making new spaces and unknown sounds out of the familiar. More clearly than before the voice recited a rhyme from a wordless song: 'dream and tree'.

As he heard this, so loud and sudden, he came to his senses. His eyes focussed; yes, he wanted to see in focus: 'reasonable', warned the voice. He fixed his gaze on the path and, to the extent that it was possible, he distinguished. Over there a footprint, a root, moss, a tuft of grass, and at the edge of the path a large rock. But a new horror gripped him – as clearly as he saw, it was not as it usually was. And the more he mustered all of his strength to see, the more alien everything became. The rock over by the path grew larger – it appeared to speak. All relations were transformed. Everything particular became landscape, a spread-out image. Desperation seized him; to flee from all of this, to gain clarity in the horror. He took a deep breath and looked to the sky with resolve and composure. How strangely cold the air was, how bright and near the stars.

Did somebody scream? 'The forest', a voice rang loudly in his ears. He saw the forest ... He ran in, jostling against the tree trunks – only further, deeper through the fog, where he had to be ... where there was somebody who made everything different, who created the dreadful evening in the forest. A tree stump threw him to the ground.

There he lay and wept with fear, like a child who feels a strange man approaching in a dream.

After a while he grew silent – the moon came and the brightness dissolved the dark tree trunks into the grey mist. Then he recovered and went home.

—

Translated by Sebastian Truskolaski.

Fragment written c. 1911; unpublished in Benjamin's lifetime. *Gesammelte Schriften VII*, 639–41; also translated in *Early Writings (1910–1917)*, 46–8.

Opening chapter image: *Little Jester in a Trance (Kleiner narr in trance)*, 1929

CHAPTER 6

The Second Self
A New Year's Story for Contemplation

Krambacher is a rather dwarfish clerk and moreover a man 'with no attachments', as he assures the landladies of the furnished rooms, which he changes every four to six weeks. For several weeks he has been wondering where he might spend New Year's Eve. But all his arrangements have fallen through. With the last of his money he has bought two bottles of punch. From nine o'clock onwards he starts a lonesome binge in the constant hope that his doorbell might ring, that somebody might call on him to keep him company.

His hopes are dashed. Just before eleven he heads out. He got cabin fever. We follow his uncannily lilting stride through the nocturnal streets. It is obvious that he has been drinking. Maybe he is not even really walking; maybe he is only dreaming that he is walking. This suspicion may arise fleetingly in the reader.

Krambacher enters a secluded alley. A dim light attracts his attention. A dubious looking tavern, open on New Year's Eve? But why so quiet? He goes nearer; no trace of a tavern: faded wood lettering above a whitewashed shop window from which the milky light seeps spell: IMPERIAL PANORAMA.

He wants to pass by but a mucky piece of paper in the window holds him back: *Today! Gala performance. Journey through the old year!* Krambacher hesitates, timidly opens the door and, since he cannot see anyone, rallies himself to enter. There stands the Imperial panorama. Now it is described with the thirty-two chairs in a round. On one of these chairs the owner – a widowed Italian, Geronimo Cafarotti – is asleep. As the guest approaches he leaps to his feet.

Great gush of words. One can gather from his speech that every evening the place is sold out; today, coincidentally, few guests despite the gala performance; 'but I knew that someone would come: the right one.' While he urges the visitor onto a stool before two peepholes, he explains: 'Here you are going to make a curious acquaintance; you will see a gentleman who bears no resemblance to you: your second self. You have spent the evening reproaching yourself, you have an inferiority complex, you feel inhibited, you blame yourself for not following your impulses. Well, what are these impulses? That's the pressure of your second self on the handle of the door that leads to your life. And now you will recognise why you keep this door closed, have inhibitions, don't follow your impulses.'

The journey through the old year begins. Twelve images, each with a caption; in addition, the explanations of the old man who slides from one chair to another. The images:

> *The path that you wanted to take*
> *The letter that you wanted to write*
> *The man that you wanted to rescue*
> *The seat that you wanted to occupy*
> *The woman that you wanted to follow*
> *The word that you wanted to hear*
> *The door that you wanted to open*
> *The costume that you wanted to wear*
> *The question that you wanted to pose*
> *The hotel room that you wanted to have*
> *The opportunity that you wanted to seize*

On some of the images the second self can be seen, on others only the situations in which it wanted to embroil the first. The images are described just as they begin to detach from their positions with a quiet ringing, allowing subsequent ones to take their place. Barely have they settled with a quiver when they already begin to make way for a new one. The last ringing is submerged in the clanging of the New Year's bells. Krambacher wakes up in his chair, an empty punch glass in his hand.

—

Translated by Sebastian Truskolaski.

Written c. 1930–3; unpublished in Benjamin's lifetime. *Gesammelte Schriften VII*, 296–8.

Opening chapter image: *Public Duel (Öffentliches Duell)*, 1932.

Dreams

CHAPTER 7

Dreams from Ignaz Jezower's
Das Buch der Träume

In the dream – I dreamt it for three or four days, and it won't leave me – there was a country road in front of me in the darkest twilight. Tall trees lined both sides, and on the right-hand side it was bordered by a wall that soared high. While I stood in a group of people, the number and sex of which I no longer know (just that there was more than one), at the opening to the road, the ball of the sun appeared faintly between the trees, almost covered by the foliage, as white as mist and without any radiating force, and without becoming noticeably brighter. As fast as the wind I rushed on my own along the country road in order to be blessed by a more open view; then, in a moment, the sun vanished, neither sinking nor behind clouds, rather as if it had been extinguished or removed. Instantly it was a black night; rain, which completely softened the road under my feet, began to fall with tremendous force. Meanwhile, I wandered around, feeling nothing. Suddenly part of the sky flashed white, neither from the sunlight nor from the lightning – I knew it as 'Swedish light' – and one step ahead of me lay the sea, into the middle of which led the road. Beatified by the brightness that I had now indeed attained and the timely warning of danger, I ran triumphantly back along the street in the same storm and darkness.

*   *   *

I dreamt of a student revolt. Sternheim[1] somehow played a role, and later he gave a report of it. In his papers, the sentence appeared word for word: When one sifted the young thoughts for the first time, one found well-fed brides and brownings [*Bräute und Brownings*].

—

Translated by Sam Dolbear and Esther Leslie.

First published in Ignaz Jezower's anthology *Das Buch der Träume* (1928), a volume that includes other dreams by Benjamin, dreams that also appear in *One Way Street* (1928). *Gesammelte Schriften IV*, 355–6.

Opening chapter image: *Revolving House (Dreh Haus)*, 1928.

---

1   Carl Sternheim (1878–1942) was an expressionist playwright and short-story writer.

CHAPTER 8

Too Close

In the dream, on the left bank of the Seine in front of Notre Dame. I was standing there, but there was nothing that resembled Notre Dame. A brick building towered above a high fence made of wood, revealing the extremities of its highest echelons. I stood, though, overwhelmed, right in front of Notre Dame. And what overwhelmed me was longing. Longing for the very same Paris in which I found myself in the dream. But where does this longing come from? And where does this disfigured, unrecognisable object come from? The reason being I came too close to it in the dream. The tremendous longing which had struck me here, in the heart of that which was longed for, did not press itself from the distance into an image. It was a blissful one, which has already crossed the threshold of the image and property, and knows only the power of the name, from which the lover lives, transforms, ages, rejuvenates and, imageless, is the refuge of all images.

—

Translated by Sam Dolbear and Esther Leslie.

Written in 1929; published in the cycle 'Short Shadows I' in *Gesammelte Schriften IV*, 370; also translated in *Selected Writings II*, 269.

Opening chapter image: *Angel Couple (Engelpaar)*, 1931.

CHAPTER 9

Ibizan Dream

A dream from the first or second night of my stay in Ibiza: I went home late in the evening – it was actually not my house, but rather a splendid rental house, in which I, dreaming, had accommodated Seligmann. There I encountered a woman, hurrying towards me from a side street in close proximity to the entrance of the house, who whispered, in passing, as fast as she moved: 'I am going for tea, I am going for tea!' I didn't pursue the temptation to follow her, but rather stepped into the house of S, where an unwelcome scene immediately transpired, in the course of which the son of the house grabbed me by the nose. With resolute words of protest, I slammed the house door shut behind me. I was hardly outdoors again when, on the very same street, with the very same words, the very same wench sprang at me and this time I followed her. To my disappointment, she wouldn't let anyone talk to her; rather she hurried away at a steady pace down a somewhat sloping alley, until she made the closest of contact, in front of an iron railing, with a whole bunch of whores, who were obviously standing at the entrance to their district. A policeman was positioned not far from there. In the midst of so much embarrassment, I awoke. Then, it crossed my mind that the girl's arousing, strangely striped silk blouse had gleamed in the colours green and violet: the colours of Fromms Akt.[1]

—

Translated by Sam Dolbear and Esther Leslie.

Diary entry, Ibiza, written 1932; *Gesammelte Schriften VI*, 447.

Opening chapter image: *West-Eastern Village (Westöstliches Dorf)*, 1925.

---

1 Fromms Akt was a brand of condoms invented by Julius Fromm, a chemist and inventor of a process for making condoms from liquefied rubber. Mass production started in 1922.

CHAPTER 10

Self-Portraits of a Dreamer

The Grandson

A trip to Grandmother's had been decided on. A cab was taken. It was evening. Through the panes of the carriage doors I saw light in some of the houses of the old West End. I said to myself: that is the light from *that* time; exactly the same. But it wasn't long before I was reminded of the present by a whitewashed facade that broke into the front of old terraced houses, which were still unfinished. The cab crossed Potsdamer Strasse at the intersection with Steglitzer. As the carriage continued along the other side of the road, I asked myself suddenly: how was it before, when grandmother was still alive? Were there not little bells on the horse's yoke? I need to listen out for whether or not they still exist. In the same moment I sharpened my ears and I actually heard little bells. At the very same time the cab appeared not to roll but to glide over the snow. Snow now lay on the road. The houses shifted their oddly formed roofs up close together so that only a small strip of sky was visible between them. There were clouds capped by roofs, which were shaped like rings; I thought to point to these clouds and was astonished to hear them name 'moon' before me. In grandmother's apartment it turned out that we had brought everything we needed for refreshment. On a tray raised high, coffee and cake were carried along the corridor. In the meantime, it had become clear to me that we were approaching grandmother's bedroom, and I was disappointed that she was not yet up. I was soon inclined to surrender myself there. So much time had passed meanwhile. When I entered the bedroom, a precocious girl lay there in a blue robe that was no longer fresh. She was not covered, and she seemed quite comfortable in the wide bed. I went out and saw six or more cots next to each other in the corridor. In each of these beds sat a baby who was dressed as an adult. I had no choice but to internally count these creatures among the family. This perplexed me and I awoke.

The Seer

Above a great city. Roman arena. At night. A chariot race takes place, it was – as a dark consciousness told me – about Christ. Meta stood in the middle point of the dream-image. From the seats of the arena the hill descended steeply down to the city. I encounter a rolling streetcar at the foot of the hill, on the rear platform ledge of which I notice a close female acquaintance wearing the red, burnt garments of the damned. The coach rushed off, and suddenly before me stood her boyfriend. The satanic features of his indescribably beautiful face emerge as a cautious smile. In his raised hands, he holds a small stick and, with the words, 'I know that you are the Prophet Daniel', he smashes it over my head. In this moment, I became blind. Then we continued to go downhill together into the town; soon we were in a street which had houses on the right side, and open fields on the left, and at its end a gate. We walked towards it. A ghost appeared in the window of the ground floor of a house that was on our right. And as we continued, it accompanied us in the interiors of all the houses. It went through all the walls and always stayed with us on the same level. I saw it despite being blind. I felt that my friend suffered under the gaze of the ghost. Then we changed places: I wanted to be next to the row of houses and shelter him. As we reached the gate, I woke up.

The Lover

I was out with my girlfriend. We had undertaken something between mountain hiking and strolling, and we were now approaching the summit. Oddly enough, I thought to recognise it by a very high pole that was thrusting obliquely towards the sky, which, looming from the overhanging cliff wall, overlapped with it. When we reached the top, there was no summit, but rather a high plateau, over which went a wide street with rather tall ancient houses on both sides. At once we were no longer on foot but in a car, driving along this street, sitting next to each other on the backwards-facing seat, as it seemed to me; perhaps the car's direction of travel changed while we sat inside. Then I leaned over my beloved in order to kiss her. She didn't offer me her mouth, but rather her cheek. And while

I kissed her, I noticed that this cheek was of ivory and was permeated along its whole length by black, ornately radiating veins, which struck me because of their beauty.

The Knower

I see myself in the Wertheim department store in front of a flat little box with wooden figures, such as a little sheep, just like the animals that made up Noah's Ark. But this little sheep was much flatter and made of a rough, unpainted wood. This toy lured me. As I let the salesgirl show it to me, it transpires that it is constructed like a magic tile, as found in many magic boxes: these little panels are loose and shift, all turning blue or red, according to how the ribbons are pulled. This flat, magical wooden toy grows on me all the more after I realise this. I ask the salesgirl the price and am most astonished that it costs more than seven marks. Then I make a difficult decision not to buy. As I turn to go, my last glance at it falls on something unexpected. The construction has transformed. The flat panel rises steeply upwards as an inclined plane; at its end is a door. A mirror occupies it. In this mirror I see what is playing out on the inclined plane, which is a road: two children run on the left side. Otherwise it is empty. All this is under glass. The houses, however, and the children on the street are brightly coloured. Now I can no longer resist; I pay the price and put it about my person. In the evening I intend to show it to friends. But there is unrest in Berlin. The Nazis are threatening to storm the café where we have met; in feverish consultation we survey all the other cafés, but none appear to offer protection. So we make an expedition into the desert. There it is night; tents are erected; lions are close by. I have not forgotten my precious treasure, which more than anything I want to show everyone. But the opportunity does not arise. Africa mesmerises everyone too much. And I wake up before I can reveal the secret which has in the meantime been fully revealed to me: the three phases into which the toy falls. The first panel: that colourful street with the two children. The second: a web of fine little cogs, pistons and cylinders, rollers and transmissions, all of wood, whirling together in *one* plane, without person or noise. And finally the third panel: a view of the new order in Soviet Russia.

The Tight-Lipped One

As I knew while in a dream that I had to now leave Italy, I travelled from Capri over to Positano. The thought gripped me that a part of this landscape only seemed accessible to those who land to the right of the actual landing place in an abandoned quarter, which was unsuitable for such a purpose. The place in the dream was nothing like in reality. I ascended a steep pathless slope and hit a deserted road, which wandered wide through gloomy, brittle Nordic pine forest. I crossed over it and looked back. A deer, rabbit or something similar kept running along the road from left to right. I, however, carried straight on, and knew that the place, Positano, remote from this loneliness, somewhat below the place of the forest, was to the left. After a few steps, an old, long-abandoned part of this area appeared – a large, overgrown public square on the long left-hand side of which stood an ancient church. On the right, narrow side, stood a vast alcove, a kind of large chapel or baptistery. Perhaps a few trees demarcated the space. In any case, there was a high iron railing surrounding the spacious square, in which the two buildings were separated by quite a distance. I stepped towards it and saw a lion somersault across the square. It sprang low across the ground. With terror, I immediately noticed an oversized bull with two enormous horns. And as soon as I had registered the presence of both animals, they had already stepped through a gap in the fence, which I had not noticed. In an instant a number of clergymen appeared, as well as other people who, at the command of the clergymen, arranged themselves in a row in order to receive whatever instructions the animals had in mind, whose danger now appeared averted. I remember nothing else, except that a brother stood before me and asked me whether I was tight-lipped. I replied with a sonorous voice, whose calmness astonished me in the dream, 'Yes!'

The Chronicler

The Emperor stood before the court. There was, though, only one table, which stood on a podium, and in front of this table the witnesses were being interrogated. The witness at this moment was a woman with her child, a girl. She was supposed to testify how the Emperor had impoverished them through his war. And in order to support her case, she presented two objects. It was all that she had left. The first of these objects was a broom with a long handle. The second was a skull. 'For the Emperor made me so poor', she said, 'that I can give my child no other receptacle from which to drink.'

—

Translated by Sam Dolbear and Esther Leslie.

Translated from *Träume*, a collection of Benjamin's dreams edited by Burkhard Lindner; also published in *Gesammelte Schriften IV*, 420–5, though with some variations. According to the editors of the *Gesammelte Schriften*, Benjamin wrote up these dreams from a number of notebooks, spanning a period of some years. In some cases different versions of them appear elsewhere. 'The Seer' and 'The Tight-Lipped One', for instance, appeared in Ignaz Jezower's dream collection from 1928, *Das Buch der Träume*; 'The Lover' first appeared in the 'Ibizan Sequence', and 'The Chronicler' was probably also written in Ibiza in 1932. 'The Grandson' might likewise have originated in 1932 when Benjamin began to collate his childhood memories. Benjamin also sent these dreams to the Prague journal *The World in Words*, but the manuscript was sent back with the stamp 'journal discontinued'. 'The Knower' and 'The Chronicler' were eventually published in the Zürich newspaper *Der öffentliche Dienst* in 1934 under the title 'Mit einem Spielzeug Staat machen'.

Opening chapter image: *In Readiness (Bereitschaft)*, 1931.

CHAPTER II

Dream I

O ...s showed me their house in the Dutch East Indies. The room in which I found myself was panelled with dark wood and aroused the impression of prosperity. But that is really nothing, said my guides. What I really must admire was the view over the open sea that was nearby, and so I climbed the stairs. Once at the top, I stood in front of a window. I looked down. There in front of my eyes lay that warm, panelled, and snug room, which I had, only a moment ago, left.

—

Translated by Sam Dolbear and Esther Leslie.

Written 1933; *Gesammelte Schriften IV*, 429–30.

Opening chapter image: *In Angel's Care (In Engelshut)*, 1931.

CHAPTER 12

Dream II

Berlin; I sat in a cab in the company of some highly ambiguous girls. Suddenly the sky darkened. 'Sodom', said a woman of mature years in a bonnet who suddenly also appeared in the carriage. In this way we arrived at the purlieus of the train station, where the platforms stretched outwards. It was called something like Oranienburg Station. Here court proceedings were taking place, in which both parties sat opposite each other on two street corners, on the bare pavement. Although the proceedings involved things including property rights, the opposite party was my brother, but my wife was absent. I referred to the overgrown, bleached moon, which bulged low in the sky, as if a symbol of justice. Then I was on a small expedition, which moved downwards on a ramp such as exists in a freight yard (I was in the purlieus of the train station and stayed there). It seemed like the Sternbergian circle – Döblin was, in any case, among them. They stopped in front of a very narrow rivulet. The rivulet flowed between two bands of convex porcelain platters, which floated more than they were fixed, and gave way underfoot like buoys. As for the second one, on the other side, I was not sure whether it was porcelain. More likely glass. Either way, they were totally covered in flowers, which emerged like bulbs from glass containers, only from spherical, colourful ones, and they gently struck against one another in the water, again like buoys. I stepped into the flowerbed on the other side for a moment. At the same moment, I heard the elucidations of a small sub-officer who led us. In this gutter, as his remarks conveyed, suicidal people kill themselves, those poor fellows, who have nothing more than a flower, which they hold between their teeth. Now this light fell on the flowers. Like the Acheron, one might think to oneself; but this was not in the dream. I was told in which place I should put my foot on the first platter when returning. At this spot, the porcelain was white and serrated. In conversation we walked back from the depth of the freight yard. I mentioned it to Döblin, the strange texture of the tiles, which we still had underfoot, and that they might be used in a film. But he didn't want to speak so publicly of such projects. Then at once, a lad in rags and tatters came towards us on his way down there. It seemed the others calmly let him pass, apparently only I searched feverishly in my pockets: I wanted to find a five-mark piece. It didn't appear. I slipped him a somewhat smaller coin when he crossed my path – for he did not stop on his way – and I awoke.

———

Translated by Sam Dolbear and Esther Leslie.

Written 1933; *Gesammelte Schriften IV*, 430–1.

Opening chapter image: *In Angel's Care (In Engelshut)*, 1931.

CHAPTER 13

Once Again

In the dream, I was in the educational house in Haubinda, where I grew up. The school house lay behind me and I went into the forest, which was deserted, towards Streufdorf. It was now no longer the spot where the forest opens out onto the plain, where the landscape – village and Straufhain's peak – emerged. Rather, once I had climbed the low mountain at a gentle incline, it suddenly dropped almost vertically on the other side; and from the elevation, which lessened as I descended, I saw the landscape through an oval opening amid the treetops, like a black ebony photo frame. In no way did it resemble the one I expected. On a large blue stream lay Schleusingen, which in fact lies far elsewhere, and I didn't know: is it Schleusingen or Gleicherwiesen? Everything was as if bathed in humid colours and yet a heavy and wet black prevailed, as if the image were the field which only just now, in the dream, had once again been painfully ploughed, and in which the seeds of my later life had then been sown.

—

Translated by Sam Dolbear and Esther Leslie.

Written c. 1933; *Gesammelte Schriften IV*, 435.

Opening chapter image: *Acrobats (Artisten)*, 1915.

CHAPTER 14

Letter to Toet Blaupot ten Cate

... $\mathbf{Y}$ou see, even my summer represented a major contrast to the last. Back then, I could – as an expression
of a totally fulfilled experience – never get up too early. Now I
sleep, not only longer, but the dreams persist, often recurring,
into the day. In the last few days it was of picturesque and
beautiful architecture: I saw B and Weigel[1] in the shape of two

---

1   Bertolt Brecht and Helene Weigel.

towers or gate-like structures swaying through the city. The flood of this sleep, which forcefully broke against the day, is moved by the power of your image, like the lake is by the pull of the moon. I miss your presence more than I can say – and, what's more – more than I could believe.

—

Translated by Sam Dolbear and Esther Leslie.

Written summer 1934 while with Brecht in Denmark; *Gesammelte Schriften VI*, 812.

Opening chapter image: *Siblings (Geschwister)*, 1930.

CHAPTER 15

A Christmas Song

Of all those songs, the one I loved the most was a Christmas song that filled me, as only music can, with solace for a sorrow not yet experienced but only sensed now for the first time.

> I lay and slept and dreamed
> a very beautiful dream
> There stood on a table in front of me
> the most beautiful Christmas tree.

But it was not only the magic of the melody which made this song tug my heart strings. For me the dreamer did not appear opposite the tree, his dream face awake, upright, rather in the song the sleeper remained and his dream stepped close to him, just as in images by primitive painters the Madonna stands by the bed of an ill person or a sleeper, to whom she has appeared, so 'the table before me' stood next to this bed. And the singing had so often brushed over that threshold between dream and waking that it was blurred and smoothed over.

—

Translated by Sam Dolbear and Esther Leslie.

Written c. 1933–4; unpublished in Benjamin's lifetime and omitted from the *Gesammelte Schriften*. Taken from *Träume*, 26.

Opening chapter image: *The Lovers (Der Verliebte)*, 1923.

CHAPTER 16

The Moon

Welti's Moonlit Night

In a wide surge, which seemed to befit primeval times, the land swelled in front of this window. And the crest of the surge lifted this knight upwards in front of the woman as once the Sirens may have appeared on crests of waves before Odysseus. Such a sea was surely strange to the Greeks. But the earth, which lifted up the knight in front of the window, was perhaps from the same substance as the woman, who, alongside the sleeping man, now corpselike, had become absorbed in this night by the distant, indistinct form. But was that the earth, whose satellite was the moon laying in this gleam? Had not its whole disc rather transposed the order of nature, so that the earth had become nothing more than a satellite of the moon, its nearby earth, on which now for its part was transposed the order of the day; the wife had become ruler, the mountains sea, sleep death?

Albert Welti, *Mondnacht*, 1917

The Water Glass

And again the rays of the moon shone like a magician's wand that reverses the order of nature. The echo, in particular, which now reached me, the more attentively that I listened out for it on the inside, became all the more a noise long-ago heard. The erstwhile seemed to already occupy all the sites of this nearby earth, and so it came that I eventually could approach my bed, when I was just about to step into it, only with the concerned worry that I would have liked to have seen myself lying in it. My worries only completely faded away when I felt the mattress on my back.

The Moon

My first walk was to the window. Through the cracks between the slats of the window blinds, I beheld the houses in the backyard. Sometimes my gaze also penetrated higher up. And then it transpired that, in the sky, the moon, with its light separate from the background of the starry heavens, stood in my field of vision. Never for a long period of time, for it always seemed advisable for me to turn myself away again quickly.

In the Dark

Slowly the moonlight moved further along; sometimes it had already left my room before I fell asleep again. Then there was a question that arose inside me in the dark; I believe today, it was the other, unilluminated side of the fear that had gripped me in the moonlight. The question, though, was: why then is there something in the world, why does the world exist? Ever again with renewed astonishment I noticed that nothing could force me to think the world. It could have been missing. The non-existent was not one jot more hostile or stranger to me than existence. The beam of the moon could alienate its most familiar details from me.

The Dream

Thus I was the prisoner of the nights of the full moon, which threw the slats of my venetian blinds over my bed cover. Once, however, the moon reappeared to me on the front side of the house. Childhood already lay long behind me, since finally we measured ourselves – like to like. Then finally it came to the great encounter.

Once, however, the moon reappeared to me on the front side of the house. Childhood already lay long behind me. But only then, never before and never after, the image of what is mine stepped clearly in front of me, at the same time as the moon. And I saw myself in this dream in their midst. Only my sister was missing. 'Where is Dora?' I heard my mother say. For the moon, once full in the sky, had suddenly grown bigger, coming closer and closer, it tore the earth apart. The railings of the iron balcony, upon which everyone had been sitting, went to pieces, and the bodies that had sat on it quickly dispersed into their cell particles.

When I awoke at night in the dark, the world was nothing more than a single mute question. It might be that this question, though I didn't know it at the time, sat in the pleats of the plush curtains which hung from my door to keep out the noise. It might also be that a reflection was its kernel, which sometimes sat in the brass knobs which crowned the foot of my bed. Maybe it was just the residue of a dream that had solidified upon awakening.

—

Translated by Sam Dolbear and Esther Leslie.

Written c. 1933–4, concurrent with the writing of the moon sections in *Berlin Childhood*. Unpublished in Benjamin's lifetime and omitted from the *Gesammelte Schriften*; taken from *Träume*, 29–32.

Opening chapter image: *Angel Contender (Engel Anwärter)*, 1939.

CHAPTER 17

Diary Notes

6 March 1938. Over the last few nights, I have had dreams which remained deeply etched on my day. Tonight, in the dream, I was amid company. People showed much kindness; I believe this consisted mainly of women showing an interest in me, in fact they complimented my appearance. I seem to remember saying aloud, 'Now I would not live much longer' – as if they were the last demonstrations of friendship of those who were taking their leave.

Later, immediately before waking up, I was in the company of a lady in the rooms of Adrienne Monnier. Inside was the staging of an exhibition of things, which I can no longer accurately recall. Books with miniatures were among them, and large platters or hammered arabesques, coloured as if covered in enamel. The rooms were on the ground level with the street, from which one could see into the room through a great plate of glass. I found myself indoors. My lady had clearly treated her teeth for some time according to the techniques which this exhibition wanted to promote. She had created an opalescent sheen on them. Her teeth toyed faintly with greenish and bluish hues. I endeavoured to get her to understand, in the most polite way, that it was not the correct use of the materials. Anticipating my thoughts, she pointed out to me that the inner side of her teeth were mounted with red. I had indeed wanted to express that, for the teeth, the strongest colours are just strong enough.

I had suffered very much from the din in my room. Last night the dream retained this. I found myself in front of a map and, at the same time, in the landscape which was depicted on it. The landscape was incredibly gloomy and bleak, and it wasn't possible to say whether its desolation was merely a craggy wasteland or empty grey ground populated only by capital letters. These letters drifted curvily on their base, just as if they were following the mountain range; the words formed from these letters were more or less remote from each other. I knew, or came to know, that I was in the labyrinth of the ear canal. The map was at the same time a map of hell.

28 June. I found myself in a labyrinth of steps. This labyrinth was not covered at all points. I ascended; other steps led into the depths. On a landing I saw that I had come to stand on a peak. A view over all the land opened up. I saw other people

standing on other peaks. One of these others was suddenly gripped with vertigo and plunged down. This vertigo spread around; other people now plunged down from other peaks into the depths. As I too was struck by the feeling, I awoke.

On 22 June, I arrived at Brecht's ...

———

Translated by Sam Dolbear and Esther Leslie.

Diary entry, 1938; *Gesammelte Schriften VI*, 532–4.

Opening chapter image: *Head (Bearded Man) (Kopf [Bärtiger Mann])*, 1925.

CHAPTER 18

Review: *Albert Béguin,* The Romantic Soul and the Dream

Albert Béguin, The Romantic Soul and the Dream:
Essays on German Romanticism and French Poetry,
Marseille: Editions des Cahiers du Sud 1937, (two volumes)

The predominant part of this extensive work by Béguin is devoted to examinations of German Romanticism. If a shorter characterisation of the French Romantics is included at the end, it is not on account of the interests of comparative literary history (from which Béguin distances himself [vol. II, 320]). German Romanticism does not present itself to the author as the mother of the French variant, but rather as the Romantic phenomenon par excellence through which the initiation into this movement of the spirit unfolds. For Béguin it is indeed an initiation. The object of study, he writes, engages 'that most secret part of our selves … in which we now only sense a wish, the wish to decode the language of signs and omens, and thus we may get hold of the disconcertment that fills the person who considers human life for one moment in all its strangeness, with its dangers, its alarm, its beauty and its sad limits' (xvii). Considerations in the concluding part are devoted to Surrealist poetry and determine the author's orientation from the outset – a sign, indeed, of how concerned he is to remove himself from the realm of academic scholarship. It should be added that he does not at all relinquish the most rigorous academic standards in his handling of the apparatus of scholarship, even if that is not the case with his method. The book is exemplarily worked through, with precision, without learned pomposity. Due to this commitment, the details here are often as original as they are appealing, irrespective of the problematic aspects of the book's basic position.

The weaknesses of the work are clearly exposed in its allegiant formulations. The author says: 'Objectivity, which certainly can and should form the law of the descriptive sciences, cannot fruitfully determine the humanities. In this realm every "disinterested" research includes an unforgivable betrayal of the self and of the "object" of investigation' (xvii). One would not want to raise any objections to this. The error only arises where one tries to align an intensive interest with an immediate interest. The unmediated interest is always subjective and has just as little right in the human sciences as in any other. One cannot immediately pose the question of whether Romantic doctrines of the dream were 'correct'; rather, one should explore the historical constellation from which the imaginary Romantic enterprises sprang. In such a mediated interest, which directs itself first and foremost towards the historical state of affairs of Romantic intentions, our own contemporary involvement in the object comes into its own more legitimately than in the appeal to inwardness, which approaches the texts immediately in order to retrieve truth from them. Béguin's book proceeds with such an appeal and thereby has, perhaps, fostered misunderstandings.

André Thérive, who supplies *Le Temps* with literary criticism in the secular tradition, observes of this book that it depends on the opinion that we hold of the purpose of humanity, whether we declare ourselves in agreement with it, or whether we are compelled to find it utterly repellent 'when the spirit is directed towards the darkness as the only place where it finds joy, poetry, the secret dominion over the universe' (*Le Temps*, August 1937). Perhaps it should be added that the path via the initiates of earlier times is enticing for the adept only if these are authorities, only if they appear to him as witnesses. When it comes to poets that is rarely the case; it is most certainly not true of Romantic poets. Only Ritter might be understood as an initiator in the strict sense. The shaping not only of his thoughts, but of his life, is proof of that. One might also call Novalis to mind and Caroline von Gündcrode – the Romantics were for the most part too bound up in the business of literature to feature as 'guardians of the threshold'. This state of affairs means that Béguin often has to echo the usual modes of procedure in literary history. One can agree with him that these do not quite correspond to his theme. This speaks as much against them as against the theme.

Anyone who undertakes an analysis, as Goethe reminds us, should ensure that a genuine synthesis is at its root. As alluring as the object dealt with by Béguin is, the question remains whether the mindset with which the author approached it can be compatible with Goethe's counsel. Completion of the synthesis is the privilege of historical cognition. The object, as it is sketched in the title, indeed encourages one to expect a historical construction. This would have accentuated more effectively the state of consciousness of the author, and thereby ours, than what discloses itself in his up-to-the-minute considerations of Surrealism and existential philosophy. It would have unmasked the fact that Romanticism completes a process which was begun in the eighteenth century: the secularisation of mystic tradition. Alchemists, Illuminati and Rosicrucians set in train something concluded in Romanticism. The mystical tradition did not survive this process without damage. This was proven in the excrescences of Pietism, as much as the theurgy of figures such as Cagliostro and Saint Germain. The corruption of mystical teachings and needs was just as great in the lower social strata as in the higher ones.

Romantic esoterism grew out of these circumstances. It was a movement of restoration along with all of its violence. With Novalis mysticism was finally able to find a place for itself floating above the continent of religious experience, and even more so in Ritter. Even before the close of late Romanticism, Friedrich Schlegel already shows the secret sciences once again on the point of returning to the lap of the church. The beginnings of a social and industrial development – one in which mystical experience, which has lost its sacramental place, was put into question – coincided with the time of the complete secularisation of mystical tradition. For a Friedrich Schlegel, a Clemens Brentano, a Zacharias Werner, the consequence was conversion. Others, like Troxler or Schindler, took refuge in evoking the dreamworld, and the vegetative and animal manifestations of the unconscious. They retreated strategically and evacuated areas of higher mystical life in order to consolidate those rooted in nature. Their appeal to dream life was a distress signal; it indicated not so much the return home of the soul to the motherland as the fact that obstacles had already rendered that return impossible.

Béguin did not reach such a conception. He has not reckoned with the possibility that the actual synthetic core of his object, the way it discloses historical cognition, could emit a light in which the dream theories of the Romantics disintegrate. This shortcoming has left traces in the methodology of this work. In its turning to each Romantic writer separately, it reveals the fact that his confidence in the synthetic power of his question is not unlimited. Of course this weakness also has its merits. It gives him the opportunity to prove himself as a portraitist whom it is often truly charming to pursue. It is the portrait studies which make the book worth reading, irrespective of its construction. The first of them, which sketches the relations of sprightly G.Ch. Lichtenberg to the dream life of his fellow humans and to his own, provides a higher sense of Béguin's capability. In his treatment of Victor Hugo in the second volume he delivers a masterpiece in a few pages. The more the reader burrows into the details of these physiognomic showpieces, the more often we will find the correction of an inherent prejudice which might have scuppered the book. A figure such as G.H. Schubert, especially as described by Béguin, shows, with great clarity, how limited the significance is of certain esoteric speculations of the Romantics, which, the more modest the yield that is granted to its immediate pickings, does all the more honour to the historian's loyalty.

—

Translated by Esther Leslie and Esther Leslie.

First published in *Mass und Wert* 2 (1938–9); *Gesammelte Schriften III*, 557–60. Also translated in *Selected Writings 4*, 153–55.

Opening chapter image: *Debut of an Angel–Heavy Being of an Angel (Debut eines Engels–Schwerer Anfang eines Engels)*, 1938.

PART TWO
Travel

City and Transit

CHAPTER 19

Still Story

TOLD ON THE OCCASION OF MY MOTHER'S BIRTHDAY

A D-train passed through a rainy landscape. A student sat in a third-class carriage. He was returning from Switzerland, where he had spent a few expensive and rain-filled days. With a certain tender care, he let his feelings rest and sought to summon up a mild sense of boredom. Sitting in the yellow coupé was an older gentleman and beside him a lady in her sixties. Unthinkingly, the student stared at them for a minute, then got up and went slowly into the corridor. He looked through the glass panes of the compartments and noticed a female student from his university with whom he was besotted – silently until now, as was his custom with such matters in their early stages. And as he saw her, he could not help feeling that this was quite natural. With the air of someone who had acted judiciously, he returned to his compartment.

In the evening, around nine thirty, the train pulled into the university town. The student got off without looking back. When, soon after, he saw the female student lugging a big black suitcase ahead of him, he approved of this scene as being quite natural. The memory of rainy Swiss days began to fade.

He made little effort to follow her through the station, this female student whom he was in love with ('after all – in love', he remarked to himself). Without a doubt she would wait with her suitcase at the tram stop. And indeed: there she stood with a few other passengers. A fine rain was falling. The tram came (not his line, as he noted), but there is nothing more unpleasant than waiting in the rain. The female student embarked at the front, and the conductor stashed her heavy suitcase. The dark mass of this suitcase had something fascinating about it. How spectral it looked, rising from the platform! As the tram began to move the student stepped onto the front platform.

They were the only two. The rain relentlessly showered his face. She stood beside her suitcase, wrapped in a thick travel coat in which she looked ugly – like some plaid monstrosity. The tramcar moved quickly; few people got on. They travelled to a distant district which was almost a suburb. Vexation rained down on the student like drizzle from the wet clouds. Slowly he worked himself up into a rage. He felt hatred for the administration, which had steered the tram into this distant area. Hatred for the darkened streets with windows in which lights were flickering. A glowing, passionate hatred of the vile, unfitting rainy weather. He wrapped himself in his coat and decided not to speak, not a word. For he was not the slave of this woman in the monstrous raincoat. Oh no!

The tramcar was moving very quickly. A sense of sovereignty came over him and he began to plan a work of poetry.

Then he thought nothing except: I just want to see how far she will travel.

Two minutes later the tramcar stopped. The lady got off and the conductor reached for her suitcase. This awoke the young man's jealous fury. He grabbed the suitcase without saying a word, alighted from the tram and began following her. He had walked a hundred paces behind her when, upon perceiving an elastic gesture of her head, he felt compelled to recount to her a few words about the time and the weather, by way of apology, as it were.

At that moment he saw the young girl stop before a door. He heard the key turn in the lock and saw the darkness of an entrance hall with barely enough time to utter an inaudible 'Good evening', before handing over the suitcase to the female student. The door slammed shut. He heard it being locked from the inside. With his hands deep in his coat pockets he walked uprightly into the rainy darkness, with one word playing on his mind: 'luggage-carrier'.

—

Translated by Sebastian Truskolaski.

Written c. 1911–12; unpublished in Benjamin's lifetime. *Gesammelte Schriften VII*, 295–6; also translated in *Early Writings*, 85–7.

Opening part image: Paul Klee's *Hilterfingen*, 1895. Opening chapter image: *My Room (Meine Bude)*, 1896.

CHAPTER 20

The Aviator

The empty marble table reflected the arc lamps. Günter Morland sat in front of a café. The cold grenadine made his teeth hurt. Violin sounds came from inside, as though bright spiritual voices were storming irritably towards their goal.

'Why did you sleep with a woman? It was a girl, it was a prostitute. Oh Günter, you were pure.'

An old woman made a fuss as she sought a space among the empty chairs. Günter examined her tiny body with interest. One could have twisted off her neck, that's how thin she was. The waiter cheated him when he paid the bill. He pushed himself into the stream of people on the boulevard. Every evening the sky was a milky brown, the small trees were black, and the doorways to the amusement halls were dazzling. He was spellbound by the jewellers' shops. With the golden knob of his walking stick buttressed against his hip, he would pause in front of the window displays. For minutes at a time he observed the hats at a milliner's shop and imagined them on the heads of women in full make-up.

He was met by a gust of perfume that came from four women. They edged their way through the crowd and Günter followed them unashamedly. Well-dressed men turned their heads after these women; newsboys squawked after them. With a hiss, an arc lamp flared up and illuminated the hair of a slender blonde. The women huddled together. As they turned around, Günter approached them with wavering steps. The girls laughed. Stiffly, he went past them and one of the women pushed her arm against him, making him hot. Suddenly he appeared in the brightness of a mirror which reflected the lights. His green tie was glowing; it sat well. But he saw himself looking dishevelled amid the lights. His arms hung limply at his sides. His face appeared flat and red, and his trousers hung in deep folds. Shame had befallen his body in all its limbs simultaneously. A stranger surfaced from the depths of the mirror. Günter fled with his head bowed.

The streets were empty and the voices rang sharply, all the more so now that it was dark. Günter Morland was astonished that during these last twenty-four hours he had not yet succumbed to some debilitating disease. He steered well clear of other people and yet kept his eye on them.

At around eleven at night, he found himself in a square and noticed a crowd of people with upturned heads looking at the sky. In a circle of light above the city there drifted an aeroplane, black and jagged in the pinkish mist. It seemed as if one could hear its quiet rumbling, but the aviator remained invisible. He steered an even course, almost without accelerating. The black wing hovered sedately in the sky.

When he turned, Günter had to sharpen his gaze to make out the prostitute he had slept with. She did not notice the look in his childlike eyes as he took her by the arm assuredly.

—

Translated by Sebastian Truskolaski.

Fragment written c. 1911–12; unpublished in Benjamin's lifetime. *Gesammelte Schriften VII*, 643–4; also translated in *Early Writings*, 126–7.

Opening chapter image: *Hat, Lady and Little Table (Hut, Dame und Tischchen)*, 1932.

CHAPTER 21

The Death of the Father
Novella

During the journey, he avoided thinking about the real meaning of that telegram: 'Come immediately. Turn for the worse.' In the evening, in bad weather, he had left the town on the Riviera. Memories surrounded him like morning light bursting in upon a late carouser, sweet and shaming. Indignantly he heard the sounds of the city, whose midday he had entered. Feeling upset appeared to him to be the only response to the annoyances of his hometown. But he harboured a chirruping lust for those hours he had whiled away with a married woman.

His brother was standing there. And, like an electrical shock running down his spine, he despised this black-clad figure.

The brother greeted him hastily with a despondent look. A car stood waiting. The drive was rattly. Otto stammered out a question, but the memory of a kiss enraptured him.

Suddenly the maid was standing on the steps of the house, and he broke down as she took his heavy suitcase off him. He hadn't yet seen his mother, but his father was alive. There he sat by the window, bloated in his armchair … Otto went towards him and gave him his hand. 'You won't kiss me anymore, Otto?' his father asked quietly. The son threw himself at his father, then ran outside and stood on the balcony, yelling into the street. He grew weary from crying and dreamily began to remember his schooling, his practicum years, the passage to America. 'Mr Martin.' He composed himself and felt ashamed, knowing his father was alive. As he sobbed once more, the girl put her hand on his shoulder. Looking up mechanically, he saw a healthy, blonde person: the repudiation of the sick man he had touched. He felt himself at home.

In the liveliest quarter of town lay the library that Otto frequented during his two-week stay. Every morning he worked for three hours on a text that was supposed to earn him a doctorate in political economy. In the afternoons he went back to study the illustrated art journals. He loved art and dedicated much time to it. He was not alone in these rooms. He was on good terms with the dignified clerk who issued and received books. When he looked up from his books with a furrowed brow, his mind blank, he frequently spotted a familiar face from his high-school days.

The solitude of these days, which was never idle, did him good after the last few weeks on the Riviera, when all his nerves had been enlisted in the service of a passionate woman. At night in bed he sought the details of her body, or took pleasure in sending her his weary sensuality in lovely waves. He rarely thought of her. If he sat opposite a woman on the tram he only raised his eyebrows meaningfully, wearing a blank expression – a gesture with which he hoped to solicit unapproachable solitude for sweet inertia.

The activities of the household were steadily focussed on the dying man. They did not bother Otto at all. But one morning he was awoken earlier than usual and led before his father's corpse. It was bright in the room. His mother lay in pieces in front of the bed. The son, however, felt such strength that he took her under the arm and said firmly: 'Stand up, Mother.' On this day he went to the library as usual. His gaze, when it passed over the women, was even emptier and more impassive than usual. As he stepped onto the platform of the tram, he held close the folder containing two pages of his work.

And yet from this day on he worked with less certainty. He noticed deficiencies; fundamental problems, which until then he had regularly passed over, began to preoccupy him. While ordering books, he would suddenly lose all composure and orientation. He was surrounded by stacks of periodicals in which he searched for the most inane data with absurd meticulousness. When he interrupted his reading, he could never shake off the feeling that he was someone whose clothes were too big. As he chucked the clods of soil into his father's grave, it dawned on him that there was a connection between the eulogy, the endless row of acquaintances and his own thoughtlessness. 'This has all happened so often. How typical it is.' And as he passed from the grave through the crowd of mourners, his heartache became like a thing that one is accustomed to carrying around, and his face appeared to have broadened with indifference. He was irritated by the quiet conversations between his mother and brother when the three of them sat at the dinner table. The blonde girl brought the soup.

Mindlessly, Otto raised his head and looked into her brown, clueless eyes.

In this manner Otto sought to brighten the petty anxieties of these days of mourning. Once – in the evening – he kissed the girl in the hall. His mother always received heartfelt words when she was alone with him. However, for the most part she discussed business affairs with his older brother.

As he returned home from the library around noon one day, it occurred to him that he should leave. What else was he to do here? He had studying to do.

He found himself alone in the house and so went into his father's study as had been his custom. Here on the divan, the deceased had suffered his final hours. The blinds had been lowered because it was hot, and through the slits the sky shone. The girl came in and put some anemones on the writing desk. Otto stood leaning against the divan and, as she walked past, he pulled her towards him silently. As she pushed herself up against him, they lay down together. After a while she kissed him and got up; he did not hold her back.

Two days later he departed. He left the house early. The girl walked beside him, carrying his suitcase, and Otto told her about the university town and his studies. But on parting they only shook hands as the station was crowded. 'What would my father say?' he thought to himself as he leaned back and yawned the last bit of sleep from his body.

—

Translated by Sebastian Truskolaski.

Written 1913; unpublished in Benjamin's lifetime. *Gesammelte Schriften IV*, 723–5; also translated in *Early Writings*, 128–31.

Opening chapter image: *Two Men, Each Suspecting the Other to be of Higher Rank, Meet (Invention 6) (Zwei Männer, einander in höherer Stellung vermutend, begegnen sich [Invention 6])*, 1903.

CHAPTER 22

The Siren

One speaks of people who took their secret to the grave. Not much was missing for Captain G to have numbered among them. It was his misfortune that he did not keep his secret to himself. For those who love wordplay, one might say that it was his misfortune that he did not keep his misfortune a secret, even though he had sworn to himself that he would.

He was no longer a young man when he let himself go for the first and final time. This happened in the harbour of Seville. Seville lies on the Guadalquivir, which is navigable until said harbour, though naturally only for vessels with small or medium tonnage. Captain G had not advanced beyond the command of the *Westerwald*, which could hold two-and-a-half-thousand tonnes. The load line of the *Westerwald* was half a metre above the water. The cargo comprised iron scaffolds bound for Marseille and seven hundred tonnes of ammonia bound for Oran. Claus Schinzinger was the name of the sole passenger.

The most remarkable thing about this passenger was the care he took to appear for every meal in the officer's mess with a different pipe, which he produced as soon as the rules of decency permitted. But perhaps even his considerable stock-pile had been exhausted during the twelve-day journey, which had brought him from Cuxhaven to Seville. In any case, it was an unsightly growth, or rather a stump, from which the smoke curled upwards as Schinzinger dreamily listened to a story. His half-closed eyes were but one sign that his entire soul had resolved to listen. For Schinzinger – and perhaps this was the Captain's great misfortune – was a great listener.

Indeed, one would really have to possess G's level of aloofness and misanthropy to keep one's interactions with this passenger as rigidly within the confines of convention as had been the case during this passage. Schinzinger, for his part, appeared not to have waited for them to connect by any means; yet his willingness to endure even the longest pauses without a hint of awkwardness demonstrated sufficiently that he was a born listener. For the first time in a long while, both the captain and the passenger sat at a table where the wine in their glasses did not pitch and toss. It was a calm evening. No wind moved through the tops of the palm trees in the large park which surrounds Seville like a belt. The *Westerwald* was docked in the harbour as placidly as the sturdy garden pavilion out of which the guests, who sat at hidden tables in the thicket, were served. Incidentally, there were few of them. Most had been prudent enough to bring a woman with them in order to be able to transform the melancholy of a Spanish song into the rhythms of their stride and their shoulders.

Schinzinger and his partner had no such avenue of escape. How is it that they had come to be there in the first place? They had barely been sitting opposite each other for five minutes when Schinzinger raised this very question. Not that he had other, let alone better plans. He was a man in his fifties and the disreputable quarters around the city's harbour no longer presented either a mystery or an attraction to him. This much, however, appeared probable: had they – he and G – sat at separate tables at opposite ends of the city, they would have been more comfortable. He had managed to laboriously prolong their consultation regarding the choice of Mavrodaphne, but their conversation soon deteriorated.

'Greek wine? Well, as you wish.' This was the last thing that G said. Then, after an unusually short pause: 'Do you know Wilhelmshaven?' Suddenly Schinzinger felt as though he had sojourned for an eternity in this town, with its ugly dockworkers' barracks, cranes and long, straight, desolate terraces, only to become acquainted with the young happiness that the man opposite him was able to draw in these dreary surroundings from his marriage to Elsbeth.

'A few weeks later', G continued, 'our afternoon class in mechanical engineering had been moved on board the *Olga*, which was alleged to be the most modern oil tanker in the German navy. Our lesson plan left something to be desired. It had not been taken into account that the examiner's commission of the North German Boiler Surveillance Association was also going to be on board in order to inspect the ship in the name of the Stern insurance firm. The chief engineer of the commission directed the procedures while our class stood waiting at the stern. The lesson, which we had whiled away by laughing and chatting, was drawing to a close when we heard voices from the midship. Some movement ensued and we realised that something had happened. I, who at the time seized every opportunity to try out my technical skills, ran towards the chief machine operator. Yes – there had indeed been an incident.'

—

Translated by Sebastian Truskolaski.

Fragment written c. 1925; unpublished in Benjamin's lifetime. Final paragraph thought to have been lost. *Gesammelte Schriften VII*, 644–6.

Opening chapter image: *Singer of the Comic Opera (Sängerin der komischen Oper)*, 1923.

CHAPTER 23

Sketched into Mobile Dust
Novella

There he sat. He always sat there around this time. But not like this. Today the unmovable one, who customarily stared off into the distance, looked idly about himself. Yet it did not appear to make a difference, for he saw nothing here either. But the mahogany cane with the silver knob did not lie beside him, perched on the edge of the bench as it usually did; he held it, directed it. It slid across the sand: *O*, and I thought of a fruit; *L*, and I halted; *Y*, and I felt embarrassed, as though I'd been caught doing something forbidden. I saw that he wrote the thing not as someone who wishes to be read. Rather, the signs interwove, as if each one wanted to incorporate the next: there followed – in nigh on the same spot as before – *MPIA*, and the first marks had already begun to vanish as the last ones emerged. I came closer. This too did not cause him to look up – or should I say awaken? – so accustomed was he to my presence. 'Calculating again, are you?' I asked, without letting on that I had been watching him. I knew that his ruminations concerned imaginary budgets for distant journeys, journeys that extended as far as Samarkand or Iceland but which he never undertook. Had he ever left the country at all? Aside from that secret journey, of course, which he'd gone on in order to escape the memory of a wild and, as they say, unworthy, indeed, shameful young love – Olympia – whose name he had just absent-mindedly scrawled into the sand.

'I'm thinking of my street. Or of you, if you will – they're one and the same. The street where a word of yours became more vivid than any other I have heard before or since. It is just as you once told me in Travemünde: that in the end, every journey and every adventure must revolve around a woman, or at least a woman's name. For such is the grip required by the red thread of experience, in order to pass from one hand to the next. You were right. But as I walked up that hot street, I could not yet fathom quite how strange it was – and why – that for the past few seconds my footsteps appeared to call out to me like a voice from the reverberant, deserted alleyway. The surrounding buildings had little in common with the ones that made this southern Italian town famous. Not old enough to be weathered and not new enough to be inviting, this was an assembly of whims from the purgatory of architecture. Closed shutters underscored the obduracy of the grey facades, and the glory of the South seemed to have withdrawn into the shadows that mounted under the earthquake supports and arches of the side streets. Every step that I took led me further away from all the things that I had come to see; I left behind the pinacoteca and the cathedral, and I would have scarcely had the strength to change direction even if the sight of red wooden arms – apparently candelabras which, as I only just noticed, appeared to grow in regular intervals out of the walls on either side of the street – had not given me cause for new reverie. I say reverie precisely because I could not fathom, and did not even attempt to explain how traces of such archaic lighting forms could have survived in this mountain town, which – though it is poor – is nonetheless electrified and irrigated. That is why it seemed perfectly reasonable to me, a few steps farther, to stumble across shawls, drapes, scarves and rugs that had seemingly just been washed. A few crumpled paper lanterns, which hung from the dingy windows of the surrounding houses, completed the image of wretched, paltry housekeeping. I would have liked to ask someone how to get back to town by a different route. I was fed up with this street, not least because it was so devoid of people. Precisely because of that, I had to abandon my intention and – nigh on humiliated – go back the way I had come, as though under the yoke. Determined to make up for lost time, and to atone for what appeared to me as a defeat, I decided to forgo lunch, and – more bitterly – any midday rest, so that after a short walk up some steep steps, I found myself on the square before the cathedral.

'If previously the absence of people had been oppressive, now it seemed a liberating solitude. My spirit was lifted instantaneously. Nothing would have been more unwelcome than being spoken to or even noticed. All at once I was returned into the hands of my traveller's fate – that of the lone adventurer – and once more I recalled the moment when I first became conscious of it, standing, racked by pain, above the Marina Grande, not

far from Ravello. This time too I was surrounded by mountains.
But in place of the stony cliffs with which Ravello cascades into
the sea, it was the marbled flanks of the cathedral, and above
its snowy slopes countless stone saints seemed to descend on a
pilgrimage down to us humans. As I followed the procession
with my eyes, I saw that the foundation of the building lay
exposed: a passage had been excavated, and several sharp steps
led underground to a brass door that stood slightly ajar. Why
I sneaked in through this subterranean side entrance, I do not
know. Perhaps it was only the fear that sometimes befalls us
when we enter one of those places that we've heard described
a thousand times, a fear that I sought to avoid through my
aimless wanderings. But if I had believed that I would enter a
dark crypt, then I was duly punished for my snobbishness. Not
only was the room that I entered, the sacristy, whitewashed
and illuminated by the bright light from its upper windows; it
was filled with a tour group, whom the sexton regaled for the
hundredth or thousandth time with one of those stories whose
every word resounds with the ringing of copper coins, which
he raked in each of the hundred or thousand times he told it.
There he stood, pompous and rotund, beside a pedestal upon
which the attention of his listeners was fixed. An apparently
ancient, yet exceedingly well-preserved early Gothic capital was
attached to it with iron clamps. In his hands, the speaker held a
handkerchief. One might have assumed that it was because of
the heat. Indeed, sweat was streaming from his forehead. But
far from using it to dry himself, he just absent-mindedly wiped
it across the stone block, like a maid who habitually runs a dust
cloth over shelves and console tables during an awkward conversation with her masters. The self-tormenting disposition,
known to all those who travel alone, regained the upper hand
and I let his explanations beat about my ears.

"Until two years ago" – this was the gist, though not the exact wording of his sluggish disclosure – "there was among the townspeople a man whose utterly ridiculous outburst of blasphemy and mad love had put the town on the tip of everyone's tongue for some time. He spent the rest of his life making amends for his transgression, atoning for it even when the affected party – God himself – had possibly long since forgiven him. He was a stonemason. After ten years of being involved in the restoration of the cathedral, he advanced through his skilfulness to become the leader of the entire project. He was a man in the prime of life, an imperious character without family or attachments, when he got caught in the web of the most beautiful, most shameless cocotte that had ever been seen in the neighbouring seaside resort. The tender and unyielding nature of this man may have made an impression on her. At any rate, nobody knew that she graced someone else in the area with her favour. And nobody suspected at the time at what cost. Nor would it ever have come to light were it not for the unexpected visit of the team of building inspectors from Rome, who came to see the renowned restoration works. Among them was a young, impertinent, but knowledgeable archaeologist who had made the study of Trecento capitals his specialty. He was in the process of enriching his forthcoming monumental publication by adding a 'Treatise on a Capital on the Pulpit in the Cathedral at V...' and had announced his visit to the director of the Opera del Duomo. The director, more than ten years past his prime, lived in deep seclusion. His time to shine and be daring was long gone. But what the young scholar took home from this meeting was anything but art historical insight. Rather, it was a scheme which he could scarcely keep to himself and which finally resulted in the following being reported to the authorities: the love that the cocotte had bestowed upon her suitor had been no obstacle to her, but rather an incentive to charge a satanic price for her affections. For she wanted to see her nom de guerre – the trademark name that women of her métier customarily assume – chiselled in stone in the cathedral, this holiest of sites. The lover resisted, but his powers had limits and one day, in the presence of the whore herself, he began working on the early Gothic capital which replaced an older, more weathered exemplar, until it landed as a corpus delicti on a table in front of the ecclesiastical judges. Before that, however, some years had passed, and by the time that all the formalities had been taken care of and all of the files were to hand, it turned out that it was too late. A broken, feeble-minded old man stood before his work and nobody supposed that it was play-acting when this once respected head leaned with furrowed brow over the tangle of arabesques in a vain effort to discern the name that he had hidden there so many years ago."

'To my surprise I noticed that – I cannot say why – I had stepped closer. But before I could reach out and touch the stone, I felt the hand of the sexton on my shoulder. Well-intentioned, yet surprised, he attempted to determine the reason for my interest. In my insecurity and weariness, however, I stuttered only the most senseless thing possible: "Collector", whereupon I toddled off home.

'If sleep, as some maintain, is not only a physical need of the organism, but a compulsion effected by the unconscious upon consciousness such that it vacates the scene in order to make room for drives and images, then perhaps the exhaustion that overcame me at noon in a southern Italian town had more to say than it ordinarily would. Be that as it may, I dreamt – I know I dreamt – the name. But not as it had stood before me, undiscovered in the stone; rather, it had been abducted into

another realm – elevated, disenchanted and clarified at once –
and amid the myriad tangles of grass, foliage and flowers, the
letters, which at that time had caused my heart to beat most
painfully, quaked and quivered towards me. When I awoke it
was past eight. Time to have dinner and raise the question of
how the rest of the day should be spent. My hours of napping
during the afternoon prohibited me from ending it early, and I
lacked both the money and the inclination to embark on more
adventures. After a few hundred indecisive steps, I happened
upon an open square, the Campo. It was dusk. Children were
still playing around the fountain. This square, which was off
limits to all vehicles, and which no longer served for gather-
ings, only markets, had its vital purpose as a huge stone play
and bathing area for children. For this reason, it was also a
popular spot for carts selling sweets, monkey nuts and melons.
Two or three of them still stood around the square, gradually
lighting their lanterns. A blinking light shot forth from the
vicinity of the last one that still had children and idlers crowded
around it. As I approached, I gleaned brass instruments. I am
an observant ambler. What will or hidden wish, then, prohibited me from noticing what could not possibly have evaded
even the most inattentive person? Something was afoot on this
street, at whose entrance I now found myself again, without
having expected it. The silk drapes that hung from the windows
weren't laundry at all – and why should the peculiar candelabras have survived here and nowhere else in the country? The
music got underway. It erupted into the street, which quickly
filled with people. And it became apparent that wealth, where
it brushes up against the poor, only makes it more difficult
for them to enjoy what is theirs. The light from the candles
and torches clashed violently with the spherical yellow beams
that shone from the arc lamps, illuminating the cobblestones

and house walls. I joined in right at the very end. Preparations had been made to receive the procession in front of a church. Paper lanterns and light bulbs stood closely together, and a perpetual trickle of the faithful began to break away from the jubilant crowd only to get lost in the folds of the curtains that enshrouded the open portal.

'I had paused some distance from the centre, which shone red and green. The crowd now filling the street was not just some colourless mass. These were the clearly defined, closely connected inhabitants of the local district, and because it was a petit bourgeois neighbourhood, no one of any higher standing was present, let alone any foreigners. As I stood against the wall, my clothing and appearance should by rights have seemed conspicuous. But, strangely, nobody in the crowd paid any attention to me. Did nobody notice me, or did this man who was lost to this scorching and singing street – he who I was more and more becoming – appear to everyone to belong here? Pride filled me at this thought. A great sense of elation came over me. I did not enter the church. Content with having enjoyed the profane part of the festivities, I had decided to make my way home, along with the first of the well-satiated revellers, and long before the over-tired children, when I laid eyes on one of the marble plaques with which the poor towns of this region put the rest of the world's street signs to shame. It was bathed in the glow of the torch, as though it were ablaze. Sharp and lustrous, the letters erupted from its middle and, once again, they formed the name that turned from stone into a flower, and from a flower into fire; growing ever hotter and more ferocious, it reached out for me. Firmly intent on returning home, I took off and was pleased to find a small street that promised to be a considerable shortcut. Everywhere, the signs of life had begun to subside. The main street, where my hotel was located, and which had been so animated until a moment ago, now appeared not only quieter, but narrower as well. While I still pondered the laws that connect such aural and optical images with each other, a distant but powerful blast of music hit my ear; and as I heard the first notes, illumination struck me like a bolt of lightning: here it comes. This is why there were so few people, so few bourgeoises, out in that street. This was the great evening concert at V…, for which the locals assemble every Saturday. At once, a new expanded city – indeed a richer and more vivid city history stood before my eyes. I doubled my pace, turned a corner and paused – paralyzed with astonishment – only to find myself, once more, on the street that had reeled me in, as though with a lasso. It was totally dark now and the music band offered up their last forgotten song to this lonesome listener.'

At this point my friend broke off. His story seemed to have escaped him. And only his lips, which were still speaking a moment ago, bid farewell to it with a lingering smile. I glanced pensively at the marks that were smudged in the dust by our feet. And the undying verse wandered majestically through the arch of this story as if through a gate.

—

Translated by Sebastian Truskolaski.

Written c. 1929; unpublished in Benjamin's lifetime. *Gesammelte Schriften IV*, 780–7; also translated in *Radio Benjamin*, 260–6. As the editors of this volume note, 'Benjamin borrows the title of his novella from Goethe's poem, "Nicht mehr auf Seidenblatt" (No longer on a leaf of silk), a verse posthumously added to the *West-östlicher Divan* (*West-Eastern Divan*), "Book of Suleika". Benjamin refers to this verse in "Goethe's Elective Affinities".'

Opening chapter image: *Garden of Passion (Garten der Leidenschaft)*, 1913.

CHAPTER 24

Palais D…y

If, between the years 1875 and '85 Baron X stood out in the Café de Paris, and if, as with the strangers of distinction, like the Count de Caylus, Marshall Fécamts and the gentleman rider Raymond Grivier, attention was also drawn to the Baron, it was not because of his elegance, his parentage, or his sporting achievements, but rather quite simply the recognition, indeed the admiration of the loyalty with which he had held to the establishment through so many years. A loyalty which he would later retain for something completely different and highly unusual. That is just what this story is about.

It begins, strictly speaking, with the inheritance which the Baron should have received at some point over a period of thirty years and was due to receive and which indeed finally came to him in September 1884. At the time, the inheritor was not far off his fiftieth birthday and was certainly no longer a bon viveur. Had he ever been one? The question did indeed crop up. Were someone to insist that he had never once stumbled across the name of the Baron in the chronique scandaleuse of Paris, and even that the mouths of the most unscrupulous club denizens and the most gossipy coquettes had never referred to him, it would be impossible to disagree: the Baron, in his shepherd's plaid trousers, with his puffed-out Lavalliere cravat, was more than a swanky apparition; there were a few wrinkles on his face which bespoke a connoisseur of women who had paid for his wisdom. The Baron had remained a riddle until now, and to see this large, long-awaited inheritance finally in his hands effected in his friends, alongside their unbegrudging goodwill, the most discreet, most spiteful curiosity. What no fireside chats, no bottle of Burgundy had been able to do – lift the veil from this life – they believed they might be able to expect from this sudden wealth.

But after two or three months, they were all of one mind: they could not have been more thoroughly disappointed. Nothing – not a shadow – had changed in the Baron's clothing, mood, the way he divided up his time, even in his budget and accommodation. He was still the noblest idler, whose time appeared as filled to the brim as that of the most minor clerk. Whenever he left the club, he took his quarters in his bachelor apartment on the Avenue Victor Hugo, and never were any friends, who wanted to accompany him home of an evening, dismissed with excuses. Indeed, it sometimes happened that, right until five o'clock in the morning or even later, the man of the house acted as banker at a green table that was just where a wonderful Chippendale cabinet once stood in his parlour. The Baron liked to play by fluke – that was clear from the rare occasions when he had appeared at the card table in the past.

Now, though, even the most long-standing players could not recall experiencing such runs of luck as those that the winter of 1884 brought. It lasted all through the spring and remained as the summer streamed across the boulevards with its rivulets of shade. How could it be, then, that by September the Baron was a poor man? Not poor, but floating indefinably between poor and rich, just like before, though now robbed of the expectation of a great inheritance. Poor enough that he began limiting himself to visiting the club only for a cup of tea or a game of chess. No one dared to wager a question. What would have been questionable anyway about an existence that took place within its narrow, sophisticated limits in front of everybody's eyes, from his morning ride, to the hour's fencing, and lunch until the bell rings a quarter to six, when he left the Café de Paris in order to dine two hours later with company at Delaborde? In those intervening hours, he did not touch another card. And yet these two hours of the day robbed him of his whole fortune.

It was only years later that people in Paris discovered what had happened, after the Baron had retreated to Lord knows where – what would the name of a remote Lithuanian manor mean here? – and one of his friends, in the middle of the most aimless strolling one rainy morning, winced in shock – he himself did not immediately know in response to what – a sight or an idea? In truth, it was both. For the monstrosity which swayed down at him from the shoulders of three transport workers on the flight of steps at the Palais D...y was that precious Chippendale piece, which one day had given way to the talismanic gambling table. The cabinet was splendid and could not be mistaken for any other. But it was not only because of this that the friend recognised it. Just as waveringly, his broad shoulders shaking, did the mighty back of its owner appear and disappear that day when he departed for the last time, before the eyes of all the waving people on the railway station platform. Hastily the stranger pushed past the removal men up the low steps, stepped through the open doorway and came to a halt, almost vertiginously, in the vast bare entrance hall. In front of him the stairway went up in spirals to the first floor, its massive balustrade nothing but a single unbroken marble relief: fauns, nymphs; nymphs, satyrs; satyrs, fauns. The newcomer composed himself and searched through the halls and the suites of rooms. Everywhere empty walls yawned at him. No trace of any inhabitants except for an equally abandoned but opulently decorated boudoir, filled with furs and cushions, jade gods and incense jars, grand vases and Gobelins. A thin layer of dust lay over everything. This threshold had nothing inviting about it, and the stranger wanted to begin the search anew, when behind him a pretty young girl, dressed like a lady's maid, prepared to enter the room. And she, being the only confidante of what had occurred here, told her story.

It was now one year since the Baron had rented this palace for an inconceivable interest from its owner, a Montenegrin duke. Right from the very day that the contract was signed, she had taken up her duties, which consisted of two weeks overseeing the craftsmen and receiving deliveries. Then followed new instructions, sparse but strict specifications, which for the most part concerned the care of the flowers, which had still left something of their perfume in the room, in front of which they were both now standing. Only one, the final instruction, made reference to something else, and precisely that one seemed to the girl bound to a fairy tale–like reward, which was now promised to her. 'Day in, day out, not one minute before, not one minute after six, the Baron appeared', she said, 'on the flight of steps, in order to ascend, slowly, to the doorway. He never came without a large bouquet.' But in what order the orchids, lilies, azaleas, chrysanthemums appeared, and in what relation to the seasons, was inscrutable. He rang at the door. The door opened. The maid, the one from whom we know everything, opened it, in order to receive the flowers and to accept an enquiry, which was the cue for her most secret duty:

'Is Madam at home?'

'I am sorry', replied the maid, 'Madam has just left the house.'

Pensively the lover then headed back on his return path, only to return once again the next day to pay his respects at the abandoned palace.

And so it became known how riches, which so often served the common purpose of fanning the embers of strange love, for this one time ignited those of its owner to the final flames.

—

Translated by Esther Leslie.

First published in *Die Dame*, Berlin, June 1929; *Gesammelte Schriften IV*, 725–8.

Opening chapter image: *Little Castle in the Air (Luftschlösschen)*, 1915.

CHAPTER 25

Review: *Franz Hessel,* Secret Berlin

Franz Hessel, Secret Berlin, *Berlin: Ernst Rowohlt Verlag, 1927*

The small flights of stairs, the front halls supported by columns, the friezes and architraves of the villas in Tiergarten are taken at their word in this book. The 'old' West End has become the West of antiquity, whence the westerly winds reached the boatmen, who slowly floated their barges with the apples of the Hesperides up the Landwehr Canal in order to moor at the bridge of Heracles. This district lifts itself so unmistakably above the urban sea of houses that its entrance appears to be guarded by thresholds and gates. Its poet is well acquainted with thresholds in every sense – except for the dubious one upheld by experimental psychology, which he does not love. The thresholds, however, which separate and distinguish situations, minutes and words from each other, are felt more keenly by him under the soles of his feet than they are felt by anyone else.

And precisely because he feels the town in this way, one expects to find in his work descriptions or atmospheric portraits. What is 'secret' about this Berlin is not a windy whisper, no vexatious flirtation, but simply this strict and Classical image-being of a town, a street, a house, even a room, which, in the manner of a cell, accommodates the measure of events throughout the book, just as it does the moves in a dance.

Every architecture worthy of the name lets its best element fall not to mere views, but rather to the sense of space. That is also how that narrow strip of bank between the Landwehr Canal and Tiergartenstrasse exercises its power over people in a gentle and conducive way: hermetic and Hodegetric. In dialogues they stride off, every now and then, down the stony slope. And just as he did with the fourteen fictional figures of his *Seven Dialogues*,[1] so here through these fragile children of the world does the author move the Roman heart to beat, the Greek tongue to speak. It is not Greeks or Romans in modern costumes, nor is it contemporaries in humanistic carnival dress; rather this book is close to photomontage in the technical sense: housewives, artists, worldly ladies, merchants and intellectuals are sharply overlapped by the shadowy outlines of Platonic and Menandric mask-wearers.

For this secret Berlin is the stage of an Alexandrine musical comedy. It inherits from Greek drama the unity of place and

---

1 Franz Hessel, *Seven Dialogues*, with seven etchings by Renée Sintenis, Berlin, 1924.

time: in twenty-four hours the entanglements of love are knotted and untied. From philosophy it inherits the great abrogated question of morality, which previously the poet has treated in its Classical formulation – with a piece of verse about the Matron of Ephesus.[2] From the Greek language it inherited its musical instrumentation. Today there is no author who approaches the Germano-Greek inclination to composite words more freely and with more understanding than this one. In his mouth the words become magnets, which irresistibly attract other words. His prose is shot through with such magnetic chains. He knows that a beauty can be 'northernblonde', a cashier can be a 'seatedgoddess', the widow of a barber can be 'cakebeautiful', a bland do-gooder can be a 'donothingevil' and a dwarf can be a 'gladlysmall'.

In another sense, however, the lovers who wander through this novel and who are never twosomes, but are always, always hemmed by friends, are only links in a well-placed, magnetic chain. And whether we are here or there reminded of the story of *The Magic Swan* or the tune of the rat catcher – Clemens Kestner is, here, the name of that rat catcher – it remains the case that, however un-exemplary each individual may be, however unenviable his path through life, this procession of young people from Berlin pulls the reader along behind it on the narrow street alongside the bank, past the 'bank-side landscape with the curved pedestrian bridge, the forked branches of the chestnut tree and the three weeping willows', which have 'something Far Eastern about them, as do too, in certain moments, a few of the small lakes of the Mark'.

From where stems the narrator's gift to expand the tiny territory of his story so mysteriously with all the perspectives of

---

2 Franz Hessel, *The Widow of Ephesus: Dramatic Poem in Two Scenes*, Berlin, 1925.

distance and past times? In a generation of poets, barely one of whom remained untouched by the appearance of Stefan George, Hessel put the years to good use with mythological studies, Homer and translating, while for others the years disappeared into the spread of dogmas, in the context of an already wobbly structure of education. Whoever understands how to read his books senses how – between the walls of aging cities, the ruins of the past century – they all conjure up antiquity. Yet even if the far-flung circles of his life and work traverse Greece, Paris and Italy, the needle of his compass always rests in his parlour at Tiergarten, which his friends seldom enter without knowing of the risks of being transformed into a hero.

—

Translated by Esther Leslie.

First published in *Die Literarische Welt*, 9 December 1927; *Gesammelte Schriften III*, 82–4; also translated in *Selected Writings 2.1*, 69–71.

Opening chapter image: *Cat Lurking (Katze Lauert)*, 1939.

CHAPTER 26

Review: Detective Novels, on Tour

Very few people on the train read books which they have taken from their shelf at home, preferring, instead, to buy something that presents itself at the last minute. They mistrust the appeal of novels that have been earmarked in advance, and rightly so. Furthermore, they may set store by making their purchase from the colourfully decorated trolley right on the tarmac of the platform. After all, everyone knows the cult to

which it bids. At one time or another everyone has reached
for the swaying tomes that it displays, less out of a pleasure in
reading them than out of the dim sense of doing something
to please the gods of the railway. He who buys there knows
that the coins which he consecrates to this offertory box rec-
ommend him to the protection of the boiler god who glows
through the night, to the smoke Naiads who romp all over
the train, and to the demon who is lord of all the lullabies. He
knows all of them from dreams, just as he knows the succes-
sion of mythical trials and perils that present themselves to
the zeitgeist as a 'train ride', and the unpredictable flight of
spatio-temporal thresholds which it passes: from the famed
'too late' of the person left behind – the archetype of all that
has been missed – to the loneliness of the compartment, the
fear of missing the connection and the dread of the unknown
hall into which he draws. Unsuspectingly, he feels entan-
gled in a gigantomachy and recognises himself as the mute
witness of the struggle between the gods of the railway and the
station gods.

Similia similibus. The numbing of one fear by the other is his
salvation. Between the freshly separated pages of the detective
novels he searches for the idle, indeed, virginal trepidations that
could help him overcome the age-old anxieties of travel. In this
way he may approach frivolity by making travel companions of
Sven Elvestad with his friend Asbjörn Krag, Frank Heller and
Mister Collins. But such smart company is not to everyone's
taste. In honour of the timetable, one may wish for a more
accurate companion, such as Leo Perutz, who composed the
powerfully rhythmic and syncopated narratives, whose stations
one flies through – clock in hand – like the provincial back-
waters along one's route. Or one may wish for someone with
a greater understanding of the uncertainty of the future that

one is travelling towards, and the unsolved riddles that one has left behind; then one would travel in the company of Gaston Leroux and, while hunching over *The Phantom of the Opera* and *The Perfume of the Lady in Black*, one might soon feel like a passenger on *The Ghost Train* that dashed across the German stage last year. Or one might think of Sherlock Holmes and his friend Watson, how they would bring to bear the uncanny familiarity of a dusty second-class railway coupé – both passengers immersed in silence, one of them behind the screen of a newspaper, the other behind a curtain of smoke clouds. One might also think that all of these spectral forms dissolve into nothing before the image of the author that emerges from the unforgettable detective books of A.K. Green. She must be imagined as an old lady in a capote bonnet, who is on equally familiar ground in the tangled relations of her heroines as in the giant, creaking wardrobes in which – according to the English proverb – every family has a skeleton. Her short stories are just the same length as the Gotthard Tunnel and her great novels, *Behind Closed Doors*, *That Affair Next Door*, bloom like night-violets in the purplish-tinted light of the coupé.

So much for what the reading affords the traveller. But what does the journey *not* afford the reader? When else is he so focussed on reading that he can feel with some assurance the existence of his hero intermingled with his own? Is his body not the shuttle which, in keeping with the rhythm of the wheels, tirelessly pierces the warp – the hero's book of fate? One did not read in the stagecoach and one does not read in the car. Reading is as related to rail travel as stopping at train stations is. As is well known, many railway stations resemble cathedrals. We, however, want to give thanks to the movable, garish little altars that an acolyte of curiosity, absentmindedness and sensation chases past the train screamingly – when for a few hours, snuggled into the passing countryside, as though into a streaming scarf, we feel the shudders of suspense and the rhythms of the wheels running up our spine.

—

Translated by Sam Dolbear, Esther Leslie and Sebastian Truskolaski.

First published in *Literaturblatt der Frankfurter Zeitung*, 1 June 1930; *Gesammelte Schriften IV*, 381–3.

Opening chapter image: *From Where? Where? Whither? (Woher? Wo? Wohin?)*, 1940.

Landscape and Seascape

CHAPTER 27

Nordic Sea

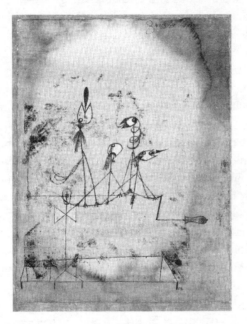

'The time in which even he who has no home lives' becomes, for the traveller who left none behind, a palace. For three weeks, a series of halls, filled with the sound of the waves, stretched northwards. Gulls and towns, flowers, furniture and statues appeared on their walls, and through their windows fell light, day and night.

Town

If this sea is the Campagna, then Bergen lies in the Sabine Mountains. And so it is; for the sea rests in the deep fjord, forever smooth, and the mountains take on the forms of those around Rome. The town, though, is Nordic; everywhere in it there are beams and creaking. Things are bare: wood is wood, brass is brass, brick, brick. Cleanliness drives them back into themselves, makes them identical to their core. So they become proud, want little to do with the outside. Just as the inhabitants of remote mountain villages can be related by marriage even upon death and infirmity, so too the houses have stacked themselves like stairs and chevrons. And where some sky may still be seen, two flagpoles are now about to lower themselves from either side of the street. 'Stop, if the approach of the cloud becomes noticeable!' Otherwise the sky is entrapped in tabernacles; small wooden cells, Gothic, red, in which hangs a bell-pull, with which one can summon the fire brigade. Outdoor leisure is nowhere provided for; where bourgeois homes have a garden in front, it is so densely cultivated that no one is tempted to linger in it. Perhaps this is why the girls know how to stand on the threshold, how to lean in the doorway, as they rarely do in the South. The house still has strict boundaries. A woman, who must have wanted to sit in front of the door, yet hadn't placed her chair perpendicular but rather parallel to the front of the house, in the niche of the door – daughter of a lineage that two hundred years ago still slept in cupboards. Cupboards, now with revolving doors and now with drawers; up to four places in one and the same trunk. Therefore love was badly provided for – fulfilled love, that is. All the better, at times, for unfulfilled love, for it must have been a frustrated lover at whose sleeping quarters I saw the inside of the door filled with a large portrait of a woman. A woman separated him from the world: no one can say much more about his own best night.

Flowers

While the trees turn shy, barely letting themselves be seen unguarded by fences, one can encounter in flowers an unexpected hardness. They are certainly not more vividly coloured than those in a temperate climate but paler if anything. Yet how much more decisively their colours distinguish themselves from all that surrounds them. The small flowers, pansies and mignonettes, are wilder; the large ones, and above all the roses, more meaningful. Women carefully transport them through the vast wasteland from one port to another. But as soon as they stand in pots, straining against the windowpanes of the wooden houses, they are less a greeting of nature than a barrier against the outside. When the sun breaks through, all comfort ceases. One probably cannot say in Norwegian that the sun means well. It uses the moment of its cloudless reign despotically. For ten months of the year everything here belongs to darkness. Once the sun comes, it roars, snatching things from the night into its possession; in gardens, it roll-calls the colours – blue, red and yellow – the sheer guard of the flowers, shaded by no canopy.

Furniture

To learn anything about the ancient inhabitants by looking at their ships, one ought to at least know how to row. In Oslo there are two Viking ships to see, but whoever cannot row is better off contemplating the chairs to be found in the Museum of Folklore, not far from one of the ships. Anyone can sit, and some will come to see in those chairs what really matters. It is a huge mistake to think that back and armrests were originally there for comfort. They are enclosures, namely of the space the sitter occupies. Among these wooden structures from the earliest of times was one whose improbably spacious seat was surrounded by a fence, as if the buttocks were an abounding quantity that needed to be reined in. Whoever sat there, did so for many. All the surfaces of the ancient seats are closer to the floor than ours are. How much more importance, however, is attached to this smaller gap, while, at the same time, the surface stands in for the soil. One can recognise in all of these seats how much they determined each time the posture, knowledge, esteem and counsel of those who would sit upon them. Take this seat, for example: a small, very low stool, the seat, a trough, the back, a trough, everything pushes, surges forward. It was as if fate had flushed he who sat here into the room. Or the armchair with the chest under the seat. Not a fine piece of furniture, rather an intrusive one; the seat of a poor man perhaps – but whoever sat there knew what Pascal later recognised: 'No one dies so poor that he leaves nothing behind.' And that throne there: behind the circular seat without arm supports towers the smooth, polished, concave arch of the backrest like the apse of a Romanesque cathedral, from whose height the enthroned looks down. In these regions, which welcomed the fine arts – sculpture and painting – later than all others, the building spirit has defined the furniture – cupboard, table, and bed, down to the lowliest stool. They all are aloof; and in them live still to this day, as genius loci, occupants by whom they were truly possessed centuries ago.

Light

The streets of Svolvær are empty. And behind the windows the paper blinds are lowered. Are the people sleeping? It is after midnight. From one house come voices; from another, the sounds of a meal. And every sound that reverberates across the street makes this night turn into a day that is not in the calendar. You have entered the warehouse of time and you look upon the stacks of unused days, which the earth put, millennia ago, on ice. A person uses up their day in twenty-four hours – the earth uses up its own only every half year. This is why things remained intact. Neither time nor hands have touched the shrubs in the windless garden and the boats on the smooth water. Two twilights meet over them, splitting into their domains as clouds do, and send you home empty-handed.

Gulls

In the evening, the heart heavy as lead, full of trepidation, on deck. At length I track the play of gulls. There is always one sitting on the tallest mast, tracing the oscillation, which it jerkily sketches into the sky. But it is never one and the same for long. Another comes, with two beats of its wings, it has – I don't know – invited or chased off the other. Until, all at once, the masthead is empty. But the gulls have not stopped following the ship. Conspicuous as ever, they trace their circles. It is something else that brings order among them. The sun has long since gone down; in the East it is very dark. The ship sails southwards. Some brightness remains in the West. Whatever befell the birds – or me? – happened on the strength of the place, which I so commandingly, so lonely in the middle of the quarterdeck, chose for myself out of melancholy. All at once there were two tribes of gulls, one of the East, one of the West, left and right, so very varied that the name 'gulls' fell away from them. The birds on the left retained against the background of the dying sky something of their brightness, bolting up and down with every turn, tolerating or avoiding each other and weaving in front of me an uninterrupted, ineffably shifting series of symbols, seemingly unceasingly; a whole, unspeakably variable, fleeting mesh of wings – but a legible one. Only I slipped, finding myself invariably anew with the others on the right. Here nothing more was lying ahead of me, nothing spoke to me. No sooner had I observed those in the East than they – in flight against a last shimmer, a few deep black, sharp wings – lost themselves in the distance and came around, so that I could no longer describe their procession. So completely did it seize me that I returned to myself – blackened from what I had suffered, a silent host of wings – from the distance. On the left everything had still to unravel itself and my fate hung on every wingflap; the right was already of the past, a single silent wave. This counterplay lasted a long time, until I myself was only the threshold, over which the unnameable messengers exchanged black and white in the air.

Statues

A chamber with moss green walls. All four are covered with statues. In between, a few decorated beams, which through traces of gold upon traces of colour let 'Jason' or 'Brussels' or 'Malvina' be deciphered. On the left-hand side, as one enters, a wooden figurine, a kind of schoolmaster in robes, a tricorne on his head. He has his left forearm instructively raised, but just below the elbow it breaks off; the right hand and the left foot are also missing. A nail goes through the man, who stares stiffly upwards. Coarse, plain, ordinary crates line the walls. On some is written 'Lifebelt'; on most, nothing at all. One can measure out the room with them. Two or three crates along, and there a towering woman in a richly adorned white formal dress, which lets her ample bosom half free. Upon this mighty base, a full wooden neck. Full cracked lips. Beneath the belt, two holes. One through the pubic bone, one deeper in the bulky robe that lets no legs be discerned. Like her, all the figures around her grow out of vague, hardly articulated forms. They are on a bad footing with the floor, their support lies in their back. All colourful between the faded, cracked busts and statues stands another one, unblemished by all weathering, his yellow coat lined with green, his red robe stitched with blue, his sword green and grey, his horn yellow, he wears a Phrygian cap and, squinting, he holds his hand over his eyes – Heimdallr. And again another female figure, even more lady-like than the first. An Allonge wig lets its curls fall over a blue bodice. Instead of arms, volutes. To imagine the man who gathered them all, gathered around him, who had sought them over lands and seas, in the knowledge that only in him would they find, only in them would he find rest. No lover of fine art, no, but a traveller who sought fortune in the remote distance, as it was once to be found in the home, and then later made his home among those most mistreated by distance and journey. They all, faces weathered by salty tears, gazes directed upwards from crushed, wooden caves, arms, when still there, imploringly crossed over the chest – who are they? – so unspeakably helpless and protesting – these Niobes of the Sea? Or its Maenads? For they stormed over whiter combs than those of Thrace and were beaten by wilder paws than the beasts, the following of Artemis – they, the galleons. They are galleons. They stand in the chamber of the galleons in the Maritime Museum in Oslo.

But right in the middle of the chamber rises a ship's wheel on a platform. Will even here these travellers find no rest, and should it be out with them again into the beating of the waves, which is eternal like hellfire?

—

Translated by Sam Dolbear and Antonia Grousdanidou.

The drafting of this cycle was concluded on 15 August 1930 and published in the *Frankfurter Zeitung*, 18 September 1930. *Gesammelte Schriften IV*, 383–7.

Opening chapter image: *The Chirping Machine (Die Zwitscher-Maschine)*, 1922.

CHAPTER 28

Tales Out of Loneliness

The Wall

I had lived for a few months in an eyrie on Spanish soil. I often resolved to wander at some point in the vicinity, which was edged by a wreath of severe ridges and dark pine woods. In between lay hidden villages; most were named after saints, who might well have been able to occupy this paradisiacal region. But it was summer; the heat allowed me, from one day to the next, to defer even the most cherished promenade to the Windmill Hill, which I could see from my window. And so I stuck to the usual meander through the narrow, shady alleyways, in whose networks one was never able to find the same crossing-points twice. One afternoon in this labyrinth I stumbled across a junk shop, in which picture postcards could be bought. In any case some were displayed in the window, and among them was a photo of a town wall, as has been preserved in this corner of the world. I had never seen one like this before, though. The photograph had captured its whole magic: the wall swung through the landscape like a voice, like a hymn through the centuries of its duration. I promised myself not to buy this card until I had seen the wall that it depicted with my own eyes. I told no one of my resolution, and I could refrain from doing with greater reason, for the card led me with its caption, 'S. Vinez'. For sure I did not know of a Saint Vinez. But did I know more of Saint Fabiano, a holy Roman or Symphorio, after whom other market towns in the vicinity were named? That my guide book did not include the name did not necessarily mean much. Farmers had occupied the region, and seafarers had made their markings on it, and yet both had different names for the same places. And so I set about consulting old maps, and when that did not advance my quest at all, I got hold of a navigation map. Soon this research began to fascinate me, and it would have been a blot on my reputation to seek help or advice from a third party at such an advanced stage in the matter. I had just spent another hour poring over my maps when an acquaintance, a local, invited me for an evening walk. He wanted to take me in front of the town onto the mound, from where the windmills that had long been still had so often greeted me over the pine tops. Once we managed to reach the top it began to grow dark, and we halted to await the moon, upon whose first beam we set about on our way home. We stepped out of a little pine wood. There in the moonlight, near and unmistakable, stood the wall, whose image had accompanied me for days, and within its protection, the town to which we were returning home. I did not say a word, but soon parted from my friend. The next afternoon, I stumbled suddenly across the junk shop. The picture postcards were still hanging in the window. But above the door I read on a sign, which I had missed before, 'Sebastiano Vinez', painted in red letters. The painter had added a sugar cone and some bread.

The Pipe

On a walk, in the company of a married couple who were friends of mine, I came close to the house I was occupying on the island. I felt like lighting my pipe. I reached for it and, as I didn't find it in its usual place, it seemed opportune to fetch it from my room, where I assumed it must be laying upon the table. With a few words I invited the friend to go on with his wife, while I collected the missing item. I turned around; but I had barely gone ten steps, when I felt, upon searching, the pipe in my pocket. And so it came to pass that the others saw me again with clouds of smoke thrusting from the pipe before even a whole minute had passed. 'Yes it really was on the table', I explained, prompted by an incomprehensible whim. Something arose in the man's face resembling someone who has just woken from a deep sleep, having not yet worked out where he actually is. We walked on, and the conversation took its course. Somewhat later I steered it back to the interlude. 'How come', I asked, 'you didn't notice? After all, what I claimed was impossible.' – 'That's right', answered the man, after a short pause. 'I did want to say something. But then I thought to myself: it must be true. Why should he lie to me?'

The Light

For the first time I was alone with my beloved in an unfamiliar village. I waited in front of my night's lodgings, which weren't hers. We still wanted to take an evening walk. While waiting, I walked up and down the village street. There I saw in the distance, between trees, a light. 'This light', so I thought to myself, 'says nothing to those who have it before their eyes every evening. It may belong to a lighthouse or a farmyard. But to me, the stranger here, it speaks volumes.' And with that I turned around, to pace down the street again. I kept this up for some time, and whenever I turned back after a while, the light, between the trees, lured my gaze. But there came a moment when it requested that I stop. That was shortly before the beloved found me again. I turned myself around once more and realised: the light that I had spotted over the flat earth had been the moon, moving slowly up over the distant tree tops.

—

Translated by Sam Dolbear and Esther Leslie.

Unpublished in Benjamin's lifetime; *Gesammelte Schriften IV*, 755–7. Also translated in *Walter Benjamin's Archive*. According to the notes in the *Gesammelte Schriften*, Gershom Scholem claimed these stories were probably written between 1932 and 1933. The arrangement of the three texts cannot, however, be guaranteed.

Opening chapter image: *Knauer Drummed (Knauer Paukt)*, 1940.

CHAPTER 29

The Voyage of The Mascot

This is one of those tales that one gets to hear out on the sea, for which the ship's hull is the proper soundboard and the machine's pounding is the best accompaniment, and of which one should not ask whence it hails.

It was, so my friend the radio operator recounted, after the end of the war, when some ship owners got the idea of bringing back to the homeland the sailing vessels and saltpetre ships which had been caught off guard in Chile by the catastrophe. The legal situation was simple: the ships had remained German property and now it was just a matter of readying the necessary crew in order to re-commandeer them in Valparaiso or Antofagasta. There were plenty of seafarers who hung around the harbours waiting to be taken on. But there was a small snag. How was one to get the crew to Chile? This much was obvious: they would have to board as passengers and take up their duties upon arrival. On the other hand, it was equally obvious that these were people who could hardly be kept in check by the kind of power that the captain ordinarily wields over his passengers, especially not at a time when the mood of the Kiel uprising still lingered in the sailors' bones.

No one knew this better than the people of Hamburg, including the Baton of Command of the four-masted sailing ship *The Mascot*, which consisted of an elite of determined, experienced officers. They recognised that this journey could come at a great personal cost. And because wise men plan ahead, they did not rely on their bravery alone. Rather, they attended closely to the hiring of each member in their crew. But if there was a tall chap among the recruits whose papers weren't completely in order, and whose physical state left much to be desired, then it would be overly hasty to blame his presence solely on the commander's negligence. Why this is will become clear later on.

They were barely fifty miles out of Cuxhaven when certain things became evident that bade ill for the crossing. Upon deck and in the cabins, even on the stairs, from early until late, there were meetings of all kinds of associations and coteries, and by the time they were off Helgoland, there were already three games clubs, a permanent boxing ring and an amateur stage, which was not recommended for sensitive folk. In the officers' mess, where, overnight, the walls had been decorated with explicit drawings, men danced the shimmy with each other every afternoon, and in the stowage an on-board exchange had been established, whose members traded dollar notes, binoculars, nude photos, knives and passports with each other by torchlight. In short, the ship was a floating 'Magic City' and – even without women – one was tempted to say that all the delights of harbour life could be produced out of thin air or, as it were, out of the ship's beams.

The captain, one of those seamen who combined only a little school-learning with much worldly wisdom, kept his nerve under these uncomfortable circumstances and he did not lose it even when one afternoon – it might have been just off Dover – Frieda, a well-built girl from Saint Pauli with a bad reputation and a cigarette in her mouth, appeared on the boat's stern. Undoubtedly there were people on board who knew where she had previously been stowed; what's more, these people were clear on the measures that were to be taken were they to receive instructions from above to remove the excess passenger.

From this point onwards, the nightly business was even more worth seeing. But it would not have been 1919 if politics had not been added to the list of on-board divertissements. There were voices which proclaimed that this expedition was to mark the start of a new life in a new world; others saw in it the long yearned-for instant when the reckoning with the rulers would finally be settled. Unmistakably, a harsher wind was blowing. It was soon discovered whence it came: it was a certain Schwinning, a tall chap of limp posture who wore his red hair parted and of whom nothing was known, except that he had travelled as a cabin attendant on various shipping routes and that he was well versed in the trade secrets of the Finnish bootleggers.

Initially he had kept to himself, but now one encountered him at every turn. Whoever listened to him had to concede that they were dealing with a shrewd agitator. And who did *not* listen in when he embroiled someone or other in a loud, contentious conversation at the 'bar', such that his voice drowned out the sound of the phonograph record, or when, in the 'ring', he provided precise, entirely unsolicited information about the fighter's party affiliation. Thus, while the crowd gave in to the on-board amusements, he worked relentlessly on their politicisation, until finally his efforts were rewarded when he was appointed chairman of the sailors' council during a nocturnal plenary meeting.

As they entered the Panama Canal, the elections gained momentum. There was a lot to vote for: a house commission, a control committee, an on-board secretariat, a political tribunal. In short, a magnificent apparatus was set up, without causing even the slightest clash with the ship's command. However, within the revolutionary leadership disagreements arose all the more often; these disagreements were all the more vexatious given that – upon close examination – everyone belonged to the leadership. Whoever had no position could expect one from the next commission's meeting, and so not a day passed without difficulties to resolve, votes to count, resolutions to carry. But when the action committee finally detailed its plans for a surprise attack – at exactly eleven o'clock on the night after the next, the high command was to be overpowered and the ship was to be rerouted on a westerly course bound for the Galapagos – *The Mascot* had, unbeknownst to all, already passed beyond Callao. Later on these bearings would turn out to have been falsified. 'Later' – that means the following morning – forty-eight hours before the planned, carefully prepared mutiny, when the four-mast ship docked at the quay of Antofagasta, as if nothing had happened.

With that my friend stopped. The second watch came to an end. We stepped into the chart room, where some cocoa waited for us in deep stone cups. I was silent, attempting to make sense of what I had just heard. But the radio operator, who was about to take his first sip, suddenly paused and looked at me over the edge of his cup. 'Leave it be,' he said. 'We didn't know what was going on at the time either. But when I ran into Schwinning some three months later in the administration building in Hamburg with a fat Virginia between his lips, coming straight from the director's office – then I fully comprehended the voyage of *The Mascot*.'

—

Translated by Sam Dolbear and Esther Leslie.

This story has two versions, and it is likely, according to the type of paper and the typewriter, that the second version was written in conjunction with *Das Taschentuch* and *Der Reiseabend*. It is therefore probable that Benjamin wrote 'The Voyage of *The Mascot*' no later than these two stories from 1932. Published in *Gesammelte Schriften IV*, 738–40.

Opening chapter image: *Hero With Wings (Held mit Flügel)*, 1905.

CHAPTER 30

The Cactus Hedge

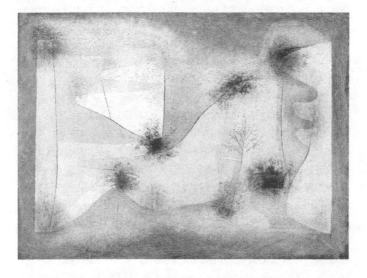

The first foreigner who came to us in Ibiza was an Irishman, O'Brien. That was about twenty years ago, and by then the fellow was already in his forties. In the years prior to settling down with us, he had travelled far and wide. As a young man, he had lived as a farmer in East Africa, and was a great hunter and lasso-thrower. But above all he was a misfit, like no one else I've ever known. He kept his distance from the educated circles, clerics, magistrate officials, and even with the natives he maintained only loose contact. Nevertheless his memory lives with the fishermen until this day, primarily because of his mastery at knot-tying. Moreover, his fear of other people seemed to be only partly a result of his temperament; adverse experiences with those closest to him contributed to the rest.

I was unable to find out much more back in those days, other than that a friend, to whom he entrusted his only valuable possession, had vanished with it. It was a collection of Negro masks, which he had acquired from the natives themselves in his African years. In any case, it didn't bring good luck to he who had acquired it. He had perished in a fire on a ship along with the collection of masks, which had accompanied him on board.

O'Brien sat in his *finca*, high above the cove, but when he wanted to work, the path would always lead him back to the sea. There he busied himself with fishing, casting the fish trap plaited from reeds a hundred metres and deeper down, where the rock lobsters walk on the craggy seabed, or he sailed out on calm afternoons in order to place nets, which were hauled in again twelve hours later. Aside from this, though, the bagging of land animals remained his passion, and he had sufficient relationships with amateurs and scientists in England so as to seldom be without commissions, be they for bird skins, rare species of beetle, geckos or butterflies. Mostly, however, he occupied himself with lizards. One can still recall those terrariums from the olden days, which took up residence in the cactus corner of dressing rooms or winter gardens, in England, first of all. Lizards started to become a fashion item, and our Balearics were soon as well known to the animal traders as they had once been to the leaders of Roman legions on account of their slingshotters. For 'balea' means slingshot.

O'Brien, as I have said already, was a misfit. From the way he caught lizards to his cooking, sleeping and thinking, it seemed he did nothing in the way others do it. As far as eating was concerned, he didn't think much of vitamins and calories and suchlike. All food, he used to say, was either a cure or a poison, and nothing existed in between. The eater therefore would have to consider himself continually as a kind of convalescent, if he wanted to properly nourish himself. And one could hear him reel off a long list of foods, of which some would match a sanguine person, the others a choleric person, another again the phlegmatic and still again others for the melancholic – these being beneficial for each, inasmuch as they incorporate the right supplementary and soothing substances.

It was a similar case with sleep; in relation to this, he had his own theory of dreams and claimed to have got to know, through the Pangwe, a Negro tribe in the interior, a fail-safe means to ward off nightmares, those tormenting visions which recur in sleep. One need only to conjure up the terrifying vision in the evening, before one goes to sleep – as Pangwes do during ceremonies – in order to be protected from it by night. He called it dream immunisation.

And thought, finally – how he dealt with thought I was to experience one afternoon, as we lay in a boat on the water in order to pull in nets, which had been thrown out the day before. It was a miserable catch. We had just about brought in a net, which was almost empty, when a few meshes caught on a reef, and, in spite of all our carefulness, tore during the salvaging.

I rolled up my waterproofs, shoved them into my little boat and stretched myself out. The weather was cloudy, the air calm. Soon a few drops fell, and the light, which makes such high demands from the sky on all things here, edged away in order to return them to the earth.

As I raised myself up, my gaze fell upon him. He was still holding his net in his hands, but lay at rest; it was as if the man was absent. Disconcerted, I looked at him more closely; his face was expressionless and ageless; a smile played around his mouth, which was closed. I snatched up my oars, a few strokes led us over still water.

O'Brien looked up.

'Now it will hold again', he said and he tested the new knot in the net, tugging vigorously. 'It is a double Flemish bend too.' Uncomprehendingly I looked at him.

'A double Flemish bend', he repeated. 'Take a look, it might be of use to you while fishing, too.' Thereupon he took a piece of cord, threw over one of its ends and wrapped it three, four times around itself until it became the axis of a spiral, whose windings tightened with a jerk into a knot.

'Actually', he continued, 'it is only a variation of the double galley knot, preferable, looped or unlooped, to the timber hitch.' He accompanied all this with swift windings and loops. I became dizzy.

'Whoever ties this knot', he concluded, 'in one go, has come rather a long way, and may retire in peace. I mean that quite literally: retire in peace, for knotting is a yoga-like art; maybe the most wonderful of all means of relaxation. One learns it only through practice and more practice – not only on the water, but at home, in the calm, in the winter, when it rains. And best of all, when one is grieving and troubled. You would not believe how often I found solutions to questions that burdened me through this.'

In conclusion, he promised to teach me this discipline and to induct me into all its secrets, from carrick bends and reef knots to spider knots and Herculean knots.

But it came to nothing; for soon it was increasingly rare to see him on the water. First he stayed away three, four days, then whole weeks. What he was doing, no one knew. There were rumours of some mysterious occupation. Undoubtedly he had discovered some new devotion.

Some months passed before we lay beside each other in the boat again. This time the catch was richer, and when we finally found a large sea trout on his rod, O'Brien suggested that I come to his place the next evening for a little dinner.

After the meal, O'Brien said, as he opened a door: 'My collection, of which you have certainly already heard.'

I had heard of the collection of Negro masks, but actually only that they had perished. But there they were hanging, twenty to thirty pieces, in an empty room, on whitewashed walls. They were masks with grotesque expressions, which revealed above all an austereness driven into comedy, a totally relentless rejection of everything unfitting. The raised upper lips, the curved ridges made of the eye's lid groove and eyebrows seemed to express something like boundless resistance against anyone approaching, indeed against any approach per se, while the staggered crests of the forehead decoration and the struts of plaited strands of hair bulged like markings that evinced the rights of an alien power over these features. Regardless of which of these masks one looked at, nothing about its mouth seemed designed to let sounds escape; the flaring pouts or tightly closed lips were barriers before or after life, like the lips of embryos or of the dead. O'Brien had stayed back.

'This one here', he said suddenly behind me and as if to himself, 'was the first I found again'.

As I turned around, he was standing in front of an elongated, smooth, ebony black head, which featured a smile. It was a smile that, right from the beginning, actually seemed like a regurgitation of the smile behind closed lips. In addition, this mouth was set very deep, as if the whole visage was nothing other than the spawn of the monstrous domed forehead, which flowed downwards in an unstoppable curve, broken up only by the sublime rings of eyes, which obtruded as from a diving bell.

'This was the first that I found again. And I could also tell you how.'

I simply looked at him. He leaned his back against the low window, and then he began:

'If you look out, you will see the cactus hedge in front of you. It is the largest in the whole region. Notice the stem, how it is woody until quite high up. That is how you can tell how old it is, at least 150 years. It was a night like today, except the moon was shining. Full moon. I don't know whether you have ever tried to take account of the impact of the moon in this region, in that its light does not seem to fall on the site of our daily existence, but rather on a counter or parallel earth. I had spent the evenings poring over my sea charts. You should know that a hobby horse of mine is to improve the maps of the British admiralty, and, thereby, gain a cheaply acquired glory, for wherever I occupy a new place with my nets, I take new soundings. So, I had marked out a little hill on the seabed and thought about how lovely it would be if I were to be immortalised deep below by someone giving one of them my name. And then I went to bed. You will have seen earlier that I have curtains in front of my windows; back then I did not have any, and the moon advanced, while I lay sleepless, towards my bed.

'I had yet again resorted to my favourite game, knot-tying. I think I've mentioned it to you before. It goes like this, I tie a complicated knot in my head, and afterwards put it to one side ostensibly and bring a second one into being, again in my thoughts. Then it is the first one's turn again. Only this time I don't need to knot it, rather I have to undo it. Naturally it all depends on retaining the form of the knot in one's memory quite precisely, above all the first must not merge with the second. I do these exercises, at which I have managed to attain quite some skill, when I have thoughts in my head, and can find no solution, or I have fatigue in my limbs and cannot get to sleep. In either case, the result is the same: relaxation.

'But this time, my proven mastery was no help, for the closer I came to the solution, the closer the blinding moonlight moved towards my bed. And I took refuge in another remedy. I thought back over all the sayings, riddles, songs and poems which I had gradually learnt on the island. This went much better. I was feeling my internal cramp subside when my gaze fell on the cactus hedge. A old mocking line came into my mind: "Buenas tardes, chumbas figas." The peasant boy says "Good evening" to the cactus pear, pulls out his knife and makes a parting, as they say, from the crown to the bottom.

'But the time of the cactus pears was long over. The hedge stood bare; before long the leaves jabbed askew into the void, before long they remained only staggered, thick shells, waiting for rain.'

'No fence, but fencesitters', went through my mind.

'In the meantime a metamorphosis of this hedge seemed to have taken place. It was as if those outside in the brightness, which now surrounded my entire bed, were staring in; as if a shoal were hanging there with bated breath, attached to my glances. A turmoil of raised shields, pistons, and battle axes. And when falling asleep, I realised the means by which the figures outside held me in check. They were masks, which were staring at me!

'And so slumber overcame me. The next morning, though, it granted me no peace. I took my knife, and then I shut myself in for eight days with the block, out of which arose the mask, which hangs here. The others appeared one after the other, and without me ever having taken my eyes off the cactus hedge. I wouldn't claim that all look similar to my earlier ones; but I would like to swear that no expert could tell these masks apart from those which took their place years ago.'

That is what O'Brien said. We chatted for a little while longer, and then I left.

A few weeks later I heard that O'Brien had shut himself away again with a mysterious task, and was inaccessible to everyone. I never saw him again, then soon thereafter he died.

I thought no more about him for quite some time, then one day, at an art dealer's on the Rue La Boétie, I discovered to my surprise three Negro masks in a glass case.

'May I', I addressed to the boss of the house, 'congratulate you on this incredibly fine acquisition.'

'I see with pleasure', was the answer, 'that you are able to appreciate quality. I see you are an expert! The masks here that you rightly admire are but a small sample of a large collection, whose exhibition we are currently preparing.'

'And I could well imagine, sir, that these masks will inspire our young artists to a few interesting experiments of their own.'

'That I hope very much! By the way, if you would like to know more I could get you from my office the reports from our leading experts from the Hague and London. You will find that this is a matter of centuries' old objects. In the case of two of them, I would even talk of millennia.'

'I would be very interested indeed to read these reports! May I enquire as to where this collection comes from?'

'They come from the estate of an Irish man. O'Brien. You won't have heard of his name. He lived and died on the Balearics.'

—

Translated by Sam Dolbear and Esther Leslie.

First published in *Vossische Zeitung*, 8 January 1933; *Gesammelte Schriften IV*, 748–54.

Opening chapter image: *Hardy Plants*, 1934.

CHAPTER 31

Reviews: Landscape and Travel

Johann Jacob Bachofen, Greek Journey, *ed. Georg Schmidt, Heidelberg: Richard Weißbach, 1927*

In 1851, eight years before the appearance of his first major work, *The Grave Symbolism of Antiquity*, in the year 1851, Bachofen undertook his great Classical journey to Greece, through Attica, the Peloponnese, Argolis and Arcadia. This journey is Classical in a threefold sense: in respect of the sites, in relation to their canonic significance for him (his other Greek journeys paled in the face of this one) and, finally, in respect of its Goethean attitude. Ludwig Klages, who was one of the first to be furnished with the manuscript of Bachofen's travel journal, quite rightly placed it in the orbit of *Italian Journey*. If what is meant thereby is that in this volume the German is enriched by several great pieces of descriptive prose, and the German longing for Hellas is enriched by one of its sweetest fulfilments, then it also means that these pages contribute nothing new or crucial to the form of Bachofen's teachings nor to our understanding of them. In this regard, they confront the researcher with an interesting alternative: were the fundamental thoughts of his later works still unknown to the traveller himself at this time? Or does that strange ambivalence, so characteristic of Bachofen's essence, operate here too? As with Wilhelm von Humboldt, the most Swiss among the great German thinkers, the most penetrating insight into the incomparability and irreducibility of any language is perpetually locked in a conflict with the dogma of the absolute superiority of ancient Greek. In Bachofen's mythologies penetrating insight into the ethnological primal phenomena of the mythical is in struggle with the cavalier affirmation of the Apollonian right up into Christianity, which was probably nothing more for him than the last world-historical victory of Apollo.

Seen from the outside, this diary falls into two parts. The middle section of the journey, which leads from Patras via Corinth to Epidauros, appears in a literary treatment. The remainder, beginning and end, is in note form. Of these notes, the editor has included only the first, marking the route of the journey from Basel to Patras. It is rather telling that, in the first twenty pages of the book, something like a subterranean groan rings from the interior of the traveller into the bliss of the southern heavens; disturbing noises, one might say, which will yet be dear to Bachofen's best readers, because they tie this youthful travel epic to his later didactic *Grave Symbolism, Maternal Right, Tanaquil.* But such reflections, as compelling as they appear, would be in the wrong place if they hoped to narrow down the rights of this book to be taken for what it is: the journey through a Greece that was by then still barely accessed archaeologically, a ride by horseback through isolated high mountain valleys at the side of a handsome Greek peasant boy, accommodation in remote villages, where under a festive night sky girls' laughter beats against the ear of the lonely traveller.

Count Paul Yorck von Wartenburg, Italian Diary, *edited by Sigrid von der Schulenburg, Darmstadt: Otto Reichl Press, 1927*

It is certainly not a pure pleasure to relate something about this book. It is impossible to berate the author, who, in the manner of a conscientious German traveller of the old stripe, renders an account of a stay in Italy that lasted several months in note form which he never intended to print. And of the editor, who in a modest, matter-of-fact preface attempts to forestall all thinkable objections against this publication, one might confirm perhaps only his innermost feeling, if one contends that these jottings possess only a few rare passages of interest that is more than private. If the personality which speaks from them were not so particularly cultivated and congenial, they would be flatly repudiated. But even as they are, the unprejudiced reader will find little striking in them. Yorck von Wartenburg was on the point of freeing himself from the inherited templates for viewing Italy. That, and how he does it, is made manifest in a historical and factually highly interesting

excursus on the mosaics of Ravenna and Cefalu. But he proceeded too shyly along what was a new route for him, such that
today – now that the renovation of the image of Italy, which
he intimated, has long been completed – his diary divulges
little of much significance. It is all the more easy to say this,
given Wartenburg's correspondence with Dilthey was already
strikingly overestimated, and the publication of this diary with
a publisher close to Count Keyserling justifies the suspicion
that the new feudal school in German feuilletonism might
count Yorck von Wartenburg as one of their own. That would
be a claim, however, which would commit a greater injustice
against this sober-minded and gentlemanly dilettante than if
not one word of his literary remains had come to press.

Georg Lichey, Italy and Us: An Italian Journey, *Dresden: Carl
Reissner, 1927*

One would have to have a card index of linguistic and
thought chaos to hand, like the one Karl Kraus once had
at his disposal, to locate this book in its correct context.

'Christ or Caesar … wrestled over a soul that was equally
receptive to both parties.' It is the speech from the soul of Mr
Lichey, which we can bequeath to the aforementioned without
envy. Unfortunately it attends the play fight on a rubbish tip,
which takes on the shape of a book.

But it is good that this book was printed. Now for the
first time we possess the ideal portrait of the 'fellow traveller',
avoidance of whom has always been the best and most difficult
part of all techniques of journeying. But will we ever manage
to shake him off, and escape the sigh: 'It is something quite
undreamt of, this Sistine Chapel'; and the admission: 'And
thus something else came along to join the shock of living

watercolours'; and the proud qualification: 'Even the dome …
did not get close to what I had seen of it in my dreams'. The
travelling mob itself here attains the voice of a choir. All who
'seek connection', who 'push their way through', 'carve their
names' – in short, 'for whom it has been an experience' – have
once and for all found a voice in this book.

'Italy! Is to attempt this theme not like taking owls to
Athens?'

It is, however, astonishing how the author would care to
attune the reader harmonically to everything that is distant
through a single motto:

> If even things take on many thousands of forms,
> For you, there is only one, mine, proclaimed.
> Goethe: Faust

The verse is by Stefan George, *Faust* is by Goethe. The whole,
though, is by Mr Lichey, to whom, as he himself explains
nicely, 'only the whole and always only the whole' floats before
his eyes.

We will furnish him with a whole!

Rudolf Borchardt, ed., The German in the Landscape, *Munich:
Publishing House of Bremer Press, 1927*

The series of anthologies from the Bremer Press takes
on ever more clearly a great, uniform character, which
appears as a most pleasing contrast to almost everything
which had existed in this form until now. For if the odium of
plundering – the unauthorised exploitation of a virginal stock
– always sticks to the usual florilegia and selections, whether
they are popularising, modernising, aestheticizing, on this one

there rests a visible blessing. Visible in the sense that these volumes, and what they bring, connect a greatness to a new form, which is now not in an abstract sense 'historical', but an unmediated, if also a more considerate, well-fortified continuation of the blossoming of antiquity. What is effected here is the effectuation of original literature itself, and it belongs in the sphere of the lives of the great, just as much as translations of their writings and commentaries on them. Nothing in them serves the abstract vagueness of education, and in the grounded consciousness of it here Borchardt pronounces for the first time on the spirit of this collection:

> They are not objective, as one says, or a listing of objects, without time, without style, without will, and fundamentally without cause; cause and time, will and style are unremittingly at work in them in the stillness, they are a part of them. We bequeath to the nation, as we sons of the nineteenth century believe in the powers of the personality, never objects as objects, but always rather only illustrations of objects, illustratively, only forms, which the object in its passage through the organic spirit has received transmutingly, and bequeath thereby, in ever-new modifications and applications, ever-new images of this organic spirit itself. Therefore these collections cannot have intended to compete with any others that currently exist, and they are moreover not at all to be compared with them.

They are anthologies in the highest sense, wreaths like that of Meleager of Gadara, whose blossoms, whether or not we even know them all by name, we now no longer think of them as dispersed.

To communicate this higher unity outside of the book, in which it is perceptible, as fundamentally distilled, that would of course be not, and all the less for the volume under discussion, a matter of an obliging improvisation. The four main views of the body of the earth which revealed themselves to Germans in the nineteenth century – the strictly geographical, the description in terms of natural philosophy, portrayal as landscape and the historical – are all combined in this book. To develop how this is done would mean writing a second one. Here it must suffice to pronounce how certain passages of the work recombine into a spiritual landscape (the loveliest one of which, perhaps, is towards the middle, where Kleist, Immermann, Schinkel, Ludwig Richter and Annette von Droste follow each other). Indeed the whole is a Platonic landscape, a *topos hyperouranios*, in which lie perceptibly and as primal images towns, provinces and forgotten corners of the planet.

Like the predominance of such general concepts as sclerotization, the form of viable opinions (ideas) makes itself felt within the linguistic as enlivenment. Therefore here, as elsewhere, the cultural historical work of this press is so little separable from its literary output. In this volume, whose linguistic *niveau* represents a high plateau without threshold, however, the poetic prose retreats so much in the face of the scientific descriptive, the scientifically constructive, it is the case that of all the remarkable sections the most brilliant might be the 'Curland Spit', a sketch of the homeland of the lawyer Passarge. Certainly those poets are not lacking here who have forever combined their image with a landscape, unless they had, like Eichendorff or Jean Paul, lost their outlines against the lyrically glowing skies. But precisely a reader who completely overlooks these isolated appearances of poets might yet ask himself whether the stylistic and sensuous peculiarities of French, English, Italian prose writers just as clearly emerge from the landscape book. So clearly do they emerge from these texts, as from these German self-portraits, the head of the writer appears blessed and peaceful, with a gazing eye, in front of a fine background landscape, and collecting all of its features in his. Did he never think about how thoroughly safe German reflection on landscape and language, and how heatedly that on state and people, has always turned out? And, he might ask himself, is the obvious isolation of the best Germans everywhere – who lack an environment of like minds, a popularly rooted, established perspective on the past – not so much a reason for his strict existence in a landscape overstuffed with experience as it is an expression of it?

But this book would not be strict about exactness, not edifying on all the scholarly material – above all, it would not be a German thing – if its fullness did not come from its lack, if each landscape's circuit, which here the historian and researcher measure, were not experienceable or encountered by another closely related German type as a spellbound sphere, as a dangerous, fateful space of nature. 'Interpreter', so pronounces Hofmannsthal, when he deals with this genius and his most woebegone, most calamitous act of God, 'they are interpreters in their highest moment, Visionaries – the scenting, suspecting German being appears again in them, scenting after primal nature in people and in the world, interpreting the souls and the bodies, the faces and the stories, interpreting settlements and the customs, the landscape and the clan.' That is embodied in its most lucid figure, Herder, and, fifty years later, in its darkest, Ludwig Hermann Wolfram. '*How* does nature seduce', so announces the pontifex of his lost Faust poem, 'the poet saturated with spirit'?

> Stream becomes the brook, outpouring itself in the flood of the sea
> the lowly flower becomes the highest cactus column,
> the willow tree becomes the primal forest's most powerful giants,
> the gorse bloom becomes the giant lotus blossom.

So has from the little German village canton up to that of the Javanese primal forest every form on earth buried its physiognomic seal in the writings of German geographers, travellers and poets in one century. Therefore the title of this book is more than a happy formulation: a discovery, and each reader will find fulfilled in it the hope of its editor, which is 'to introduce' a portion of 'lost German intellectual greats'.

—

Translated by Esther Leslie and Sebastian Truskolaski.

First published in the *Frankfurter Zeitung*, 3 February 1928; *Gesammelte Schriften III*, 88–94.

Opening chapter image: *Possibilities at Sea*, 1932.

PART THREE
Play and Pedagogy

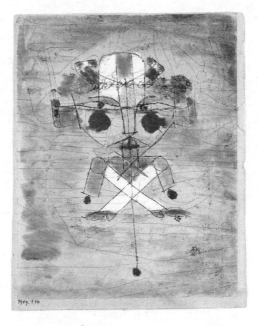

CHAPTER 32

Review: Collection of
Frankfurt Children's Rhymes

The cultural effect that children's lives and activities exert
on the ethnic and linguistic communities in which they
take place has been, to this day, a largely unexplored chapter
of cultural history, and yet it is one of the most relevant. As
contribution to this, the highest value should be accorded to a
comprehensive collection of verses and sayings of children from
Frankfurt, of which I am about to convey something. Its creator
is the locally based Rector Wehrhan, though incidentally he is

not a child of Frankfurt but, rather, a native of Lippe. In 1908, he laid the foundations for a large archive, which has grown over the course of time to include well over a thousand pieces and fragments, thanks not only to his tireless efforts, but also to a well-organised support system. Everything – all manner of verses, turns of phrase, jokes and puzzles – that accompanies the lives of Frankfurt schoolchildren, from their earliest babyhood to the threshold of puberty, can be found here, no matter whether these are the child's own idioms or whether they have their origin in stereotypical phrases from their parents' tongue.

What is found in Wehrhan's collection, however, is partly an ancient good; in only a few cases was it created by children. And the judicious user of these documents will not focus on 'originals'. Rather, here he can trace how the child 'models', how he or she 'tinkers', how – in the intellectual realm as well as in the sensuous one – he or she never adopts the established form as such, and how the whole richness of his or her mental world occupies the narrow track of variation. The children return the oldest fragments and phrases of verse to the adults in variegated forms; their work lies not so much in the gist of these pieces, as in the unpredictably appealing play of transformation. The material encompasses around a hundred folders, organised according to keywords. There are 'the first jokes', 'baking cakes', 'rhymes told on the lap', 'going to bed and getting up', 'the dumb and clumsy child', 'the weather', 'animal names', 'plants', 'weekdays', 'Zeppelin', 'world war', 'nicknames', 'Jewish rhymes', 'banter and teasing', 'tongue twisters', 'popular songs', to name but a few. This is to say nothing of the great collection of playground rhymes and the impressive codex of hopscotch games, including the copious schemes that have been drawn in chalk onto the pavements of Frankfurt, where, over the years, playing children have hopped on one leg.

Some rhymes from the World War with their scathing satirical power:

> My mother became a soldier
> She got some trousers for that
> With red edging
> Tara zing da
> My mother became a soldier.

> My mother became a soldier
> She received a coat for that
> With shiny buttons on it
> Tara zing da
> My mother became a soldier.

> My mother became a soldier
> She got some boots for that
> With high legs on them
> Tara zing da
> My mother became a soldier.

> My mother became a soldier
> She received a helmet for that
> With Kaiser Wilhelm on it
> Tara zing da
> My mother became a soldier.

> My mother became a soldier
> She got a shotgun for that
> And so she shoots here and there
> Tara zing da
> My mother became a soldier.

My mother became a soldier
So then she went into the trenches
And there she got kohlrabi
Tara zing da
My mother became a soldier.

My mother became a soldier
She got put in a military hospital
She got put in a canopy bed
Tara zing da
My mother became a soldier.

If I stand in the dark midnight
So lonely on the hunt for lice
And I think of my silent home
That thinks of me in the moonlight.

Little Marie
You silly little cow
I will pull up one of your little legs
Then you must limp
On your ham
Then you will go to the city hospital
Then you'll be operated on
You will be smeared with soft soap
Then the German men's choir will come
And sing a little song for you.

Some counting rhymes:

On a rubber-rubber-mountain,
There lives a rubber-rubber-dwarf,

Has a rubber-rubber-wife.
The rubber-rubber-wife
Has a rubber-rubber-child.
The rubber-rubber-child
Has a rubber-rubber-ball,
Threw it in the air.
The rubber-rubber-ball
Broke.
And you are a Jew.

*   *   *

10, 20, 30,
Girl, you work hard,
40, 50, 60,
Girl, you are blotchy,
70, 80, 90,
Girl, you are alone.

Some constructivist feats:

Last glove I lost my autumn.
I went finding for three days, before I looked for it.
I came to a peep, there I peered through.
There sat three chairs on a man
Now I took off my good day and said:
'Hat, Sirs'.

Lovely father from my greeting. Here would be
Soles to beboot. He does not need to money for his fear.
If he would come in, he would pass by.

An old cloister joke from children's lips:

> Dear parish of Pig Mountain!
> Stand up or remain seated.
> We read in the book of Pitchfork,
> Six prongs and thirty-five gaiter buttons,
> Where it is written:
> In my earliest youth I perpetrated my boldest deed.
> With ice-cold water I burnt out the eyes of children.
> And with a blunt rasp I cut off their fingers.
> After the deed was done the broom handle arrested me.
> This brought me to the higher regional court Burglary.
> Here I received fourteen days detention, afterwards freedom.
> Now receive the blessing of the Lord!
> The hat-maker makes hats for you,
> The umbrella-maker makes covers for you,
> The roof-maker lets his roofs shine over you.
> We are singing song number three hundred:
> Big clump, we plane you!
> Hallelujah!

Hopefully all those who are interested in researching children's creativity need not wait too long for a complete publication of the Wehrhan collection.

—

Translated by Esther Leslie.

First published *Frankfurter Zeitung*, 16 August 1925; *Gesammelte Schriften IV*, 792–6.

Opening part image: *Jumping Jack (Hampelmann)*, 1919. Opening chapter image: *Bust of a Child (Kopf eines Kindes)*, 1939.

CHAPTER 33

Fantasy Sentences

Formed by an eleven-year-old girl from words given to her.

Freedom – garden – faded – greeting – crazy – eye of a needle

Since freedom cannot be attained as quickly as the leaves in the garden have faded, its greeting is all the stormier, and even the crazy people, who believe the eye of a needle to be larger than a monkey, take part.

Table cloth – sky – pillow – continent – eternity

The table in front of him was covered by a table cloth and it stood under the open sky. He lay on the pillow on the continent remote from the world, as if he did not want to wake up for eternity.

Lips – bendy – dice – rope – lemon

Her lips were so rosy, like bendy roses, when one infected them while playing with dice or during a tug of war with a rope, but her gaze was bitter like the peel of a lemon.

Corner – emphasis – character – drawer – flat

On the corner – he said it with emphasis – I saw a character that was flat like a drawer.

Pipe – border – booty – busy – skinny

The pipe at the border was a place for robbers. This is where they brought their booty, since the path was not busy. In the moonlight, the figures appeared skinny.

Pretzel – feather[1] – pause – lament – doohickey

Time curves like a pretzel through nature. The feather paints the landscape and, if there is a pause, then it is filled with rain. One hears a lament because there is no doohickey.

—

Translated by Esther Leslie.

First published in *Die Literarische Welt*, 3 December 1926; *Gesammelte Schriften IV*, 802–3.

Opening chapter image: *Portrait Sketch of a Costumed Lady (Bildnisskizze einer kostümierten Dame)*, 1924.

---

1   The German *Feder* can mean 'feather' or 'quill'.

CHAPTER 34

Wall Calendar from Die literarische Welt *for 1927*

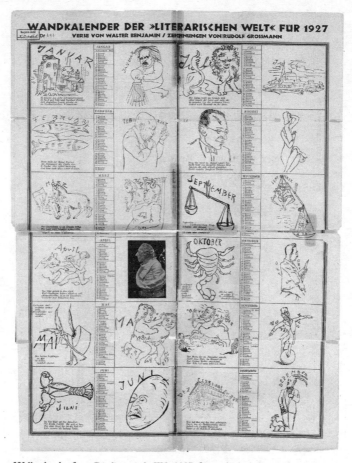

Wall calendar from *Die literarische Welt*, 1927, from which these verses were taken

Verses by Walter Benjamin
Drawings by Rudolf Grossmann

JANUARY

The year 1927 is announced
In tones to be heard in North and South
  (and in Free City Danzig).
For German readers of this almanac
Aquarius is the sign of the zodiac.[1]

FEBRUARY

Next the month of February
Presents the fishes' canopy.
S. Fischer though lives here on earth
And offers you his peace for all it is worth.[2]

MARCH

The *Querschnitt* mag is cheap basically,
Springtime[3] creeps up only reluctantly.
To the joy of every good snob
Both are ruled by Wedderkop.[4]

APRIL

April is the month of the bull,
But Grossmann won't draw one at all.
(Probably a result of some complex)
So here instead is Fridericus Rex.[5]

---

1 Aquarius is Wassermann in German. Jakob Wassermann (1073 1934), a German Jewish novelist, is pictured.

2 S. Fischer refers to the head of the publishing house, S. Fischer Verlag. Samuel Fischer (1859–1934) is pictured.

3 The German for springtime is Lenz. Leo Lenz (1878–1962) was also the name of an Austrian playwright of the period.

4 Hermann von Wedderkop (1875–1956) was editor of *Die Querschnitt*, a rather highbrow cultural magazine. He is pictured.

5 Rudolf Grossmann (1882–1941) is the illustrator.

MAY

Laurels are usually evergreens,
Writers squirt out thoughts as streams.
For the twins in May
It doesn't matter either way.

JUNE

The June animal, beloved of the Pen-Club member,
Is right here – the crab – on the agenda.
But who, you might ask, is that nought?
It is Ludwig Fulda and none ought.[6]

JULY

Bab is essentially the name of July
(the lion growls and says bye-bye).
Many a lion with polemics to deliver
Belongs to Neustadt on the Dosse River.[7]

AUGUST

Prague, which usually in August is bare,
Today bakes fresh bread from cornfields there –
Authors who all too quickly give in
Result from the sign of the zodiac which is the virgin.[8]

SEPTEMBER

September –
Libra or scale is the astrological sign

---

6   Ludwig Fulda (1862–1939) was a playwright and poet. He is pictured.

7   Julius Bab (1880–1955), dramatist and theatre critic, is referenced here. Neustadt (Dosse) is known primarily for horse breeding.

8   The German word for cornfield is Kornfeld. Paul Kornfeld (1889–1942), a native of Prague, was a Jewish playwright and drama theorist who wrote in German and worked in an Expressionist idiom; he also wrote satire and sexual comedies.

The question being –
Filth or grime,
Let us weigh it up quite precisely
Lulu or Gneisenau – which will it be?[9]

OCTOBER

Scorpio stings from his rump
Head-on, Siegfried Jacobsohn delivered his thump.
October lets us him revere
With Sternheim's astral-premieres.[10]

NOVEMBER

The man in November with arrow and bow,
is called Arno Holz. Heaven does not know
Becker, who is his rival.
Herr Külz has a tricky pedestal.[11]

DECEMBER

Quite badly crumpled is his beard,
Through which the purrs of the poet are heard,
Still (if as pacifist, he is inadmissible)
He remains, as a Capricorn, quite permissible.

---

9   Depicted in the scales are two cultural sensations from 1926: Lulu, the sexually liberated and ultimately tragic figure from Wedekind's play, which was performed in Berlin, and General Gneisenau, a military figure who was the subject of a military history drama by Wolfgang Goetz, which was performed in Berlin and was praised as a masterpiece depicting German military bravery.

10   Siegfried Jacobsohn (1881–1926) was an influential theatre critic and editor of the theatre journal *Die Weltbühne*. Carl Sternheim (1878–1942) was a playwright and short-story writer. Jacobsohn is pictured.

11   Arno Holz (1863–1929) was a poet and dramatist. Carl Heinrich Becker (1876–1933) was a scholar of the Orient and Prussian minister of culture, with whom Holz had run-ins in relation to the formation of the Prussian Academy of the Arts. Wilhelm Külz (1875–1948) was interior minister of the Weimar Republic in 1926–7. He is performing the balancing act.

—

Translated by Esther Leslie.

First published in *Die literarische Welt*, 24 December 1926; *Gesammelte Schriften VI*, 545–7.

Opening chapter image: *Flower Family V (Blumenfamilie V)*, 1922.

CHAPTER 35

Riddles

The Stranger's Reply

Some of our readers have perhaps already heard the joke which the ancient Greek Sophists (a school of philosophy) invented in order to demonstrate the complexity of human thinking. The joke is called 'The Cretan', because in it appears a man from the island of Crete, who proposes two statements. Firstly: all Cretans are liars. Secondly: I am a Cretan. So now what should we believe about the man? If he is a Cretan, then he is lying and is (because he maintained that he was one) not one. If he is not a Cretan, then he spoke the truth and so is one. It is not clearly evident from this little joke that a debate developed in relation to it, in which significant minds have participated up until our day. One of the last ones to occupy himself with this question is the Englishman Bertrand Russell, who is still alive and who devised a whole number of such puzzle questions, which are named 'Russell's Paradoxes' after him. They have a very serious background, but that does not prevent them from sometimes taking a jokey form, as, for example, the following: a barber lives in a small town, and in front of his shop he has a sign: 'All those who do not shave themselves are shaved by me.' But what happens to the barber himself? If he does not shave himself, then according to his own announcement he must shave himself. If he does shave himself, then according to his announcement he is not allowed to shave himself.

Now perhaps our readers might like to devise a joke like this themselves, and, to help them along, we include the following story:

A stranger came across a pretty garden and wanted to go in. But the gardener said to him that this garden was a special case. Because, namely, everyone who wanted to enter it had to advance a claim. If it is a true one, then he has to pay three marks. If it is not true, then he has to pay six marks. But the stranger, who was not keen on either, thought for a little while and advanced a claim that made the gardener as perplexed as the little jokes we just told made the reader. In this way the stranger gained admission without payment.

What was his claim?

Solution: The stranger, 'I have to pay six marks.' If he really has to pay six marks, then his claim is true and he only has to pay three marks. If he doesn't have to pay six marks, then his claim is false and he has to pay six marks.

Succinct

The famous Viennese man of finance L counted among his friends the actor Mitterwurzer, whom he had once helped with a loan. As its repayment was a long time coming, and after several reminders had borne no fruit, L sent his friend a ticket on which stood nothing other than *?*.

At their next meeting, Mitterwurzer pointed to the ticket and said: 'You are not only frugal with your guilders [*Gulden*], my friend, but also with your letters.'

'If you can be frugal with letters, perhaps you might also learn it with guilders.'

'That is not hard', replied the actor, 'my answer has only two letters'. The banker did not believe that possible and so they agreed to a wager. For the winner, the debt should be compensated or absolved. Mitterwurzer took his pencil and wrote two letters and won on the spot. How?

Solution: Gulden – Ge*d*ulden.[1]

—

Translated by Esther Leslie.

Unpublished in Benjamin's lifetime and undated; *Gesammelte Schriften VII*, 301–5.

Opening chapter image: *Watchful Angel (Wachsamer Engel)*, 1939.

---

1   The word for guilders, a type of coin, is transformed to a word meaning 'wait patiently' by the addition of two letters.

CHAPTER 36

Radio Games

Under the pine tree
with trembling jaw,
in pink satin
Gretchen leafs through the atlas,
and then hurries to the ball,
a ball made of snow:
'Oh woe, my bouquet,
There is a struggle'!
She threatens with the comb,
Her neck bristles:

> 'If you were only in a cage,
> You good-for-nothing farmer!'

Under the pine tree an atlas lay open, and next to it was a ball and a bouquet of flowers, which had not yet been bound. This was proof that father and mother and child were disturbed when the farmer called for help from the ridge of the mountains.

Keywords: *Kiefer* (pine tree/jaw)
         Ball (ball)
         Strauss (bouquet/ostrich/struggle)
         Kamm (comb/ridge/neck)
         Bauer (farmer/cage)
         Atlas (atlas/satin)

—

Translated by Esther Leslie.

First published in the *Südwestdeutsche Rundfunk-Zeitschrift* 8, no. 3, 1932, 5. These are two listeners' responses to Benjamin's radio challenge.

Opening chapter image: *The Trumpet Sounds (Die Posaune)*, 1921.

CHAPTER 37

Short Stories

Why the Elephant Is Called 'Elephant'

It was once upon a time. There was a man called Elephant, but in those days people were not aware of the elephant in the way they are aware of it today, because this was several thousand years ago. And all of a sudden – everyone was really surprised – an animal appeared which did not have a name and the man saw it and, because it had a short nose and looked so similar to a human being, he adopted it and it stayed with him.

And it remained with him. He picked up a piece of wood, not a very long piece, but very heavy, and threw it, so the animal might go and fetch it. And because the animal did not have any hands with which it could pick up the stick of wood, it tried to grasp the wood with its nose.

But the nose was very short and it was a lot of bother for the animal. And as it tried again and again and again – this took a very long time! – the nose grew longer and longer and longer from trying.

The thing about the name was earlier, when the nose was still short. And because the animal was with a man called Elephant, people started calling it elephant.

And by now the nose was so long that it could grab the piece of wood quite easily. And the animal felt good and got bigger and bigger. And today it is just as big and fat with a long nose-hand – yes, it is our elephant. That is the story.

How the Boat Was Invented and Why It Is Called 'Boat'

Before all the other people, there lived one person and he was called Boat. He was the first person, as before him there was only an angel who transformed himself into a person, but that is another story.

So the man called Boat wanted to go on the water – you should know that back then there was a lot more water than today. He tied himself to some planks with ropes, a long plank along the belly, that was the keel. And he took a pointed cap of planks, which was, when he lay in the water, at the front – that was the prow. And he stretched out a leg behind him and navigated with it.

In this manner he lay on the water and navigated and rowed with his arms and moved very easily through the water with his plank cap, because it was pointed. Yes, that is how it was: the man Boat, the first man, made himself into a boat, with which one could travel on water.

And therefore – of course that is quite obvious – because he himself was called Boat, he named what he had made 'boat'. And that is why the boat is called 'boat'.

Funny Story from When There Were Not Yet Any People

In those days the earth was not yet firm and everything was boggy, like wet dough. First of all there was a tree, which was massive and could run – you see, the first trees could run like animals. The enormous tree went for a walk and ran and suddenly, right at the edge of the deepest bog, it fell with a huge splash into the water.

And in the same moment, everything turned solid. The dough became quite hard, and everywhere on the ground there were lumpy stones and sticks, so that people – which did not yet exist – simply would not have been able to walk, because it would have hurt too much.

Then the angel transformed itself down here for the first time and had wings of iron and looked at the earth. And then God sprayed something very wet again onto the earth and everything turned to bog and lake and sea once more.

But it dried out in the sun, and now it was flat in a lot of places. But now there were also mountains – because the great spraying had washed away the sand and made creases and folds – mountains, to be precise. When I spray, only little creases and lakes appear. If God sprays, then mountains appear.

And the angel, who was now walking down below, allowed his wings to melt and then they were gone and the angel was a person. But there were still lumps on the ground – like modelling sand. It bonded.

That is what the people were made from – first the gentleman who was called Boat. They formed themselves – they simply became. The angel, who had also become a human, only needed to watch. They made themselves in his image.

Then the people built breakwaters and put up lots of monuments and iron men with broadly outspanned wings on them. But this was much later, a short time before they invented lamps.

—

Translated by Esther Leslie.

Written 26 September 1933; unpublished in Benjamin's lifetime. *Gesammelte Schriften VII*, 298–300.

Opening chapter image: *What He Lacks (Was Fehlt Ihm?)*, 1930.

CHAPTER 38

Four Tales

The Warning

At a place famous for day trips, not far from Qīngdǎo, there was a section of rock which stood out on account of its romantic location and the steep cliff walls that dropped off into the depths. This wall of rock was the destination of many love-struck men during the happy phase, and, after each had admired the landscape arm in arm with his girl, they would stop for a bite to eat, accompanied by the same, at a nearby restaurant. This restaurant was doing very well. It belonged to Mr Ming.

Then one day a lover who had been abandoned got the idea of ending his life in exactly the same place where he had enjoyed it to the fullest, and so, close to the restaurant, he flung himself from the rock into the depths. This inventive lover found imitators, and it wasn't long before this section of rock became as equally renowned as a place of skulls.

Through this new reputation, though, Mr Ming's establishment suffered; no cavalier dared to take his lady to a place where he had to be prepared to see an ambulance arrive at any time. Mr Ming's business got worse and worse, and there was nothing left for him except to think out a plan. One day he shut himself in his room. When he re-emerged, he went promptly to the nearby electricity station. After a few days a wire appeared, stretched along the outer edge of the romantic section of rock. A board hanging from it bore the words: 'Danger! High voltage! Risk of Death!' Since then, those contemplating suicide avoided this area, and Mr Ming's business flourished as it did in former times.

The Signature

Potemkin suffered from severe, more or less regularly recurring bouts of depression, during which no one was allowed to go near him, and access to his chamber was strictly forbidden. This suffering was never mentioned at the court, in particular everyone knew that any reference to it would attract the disfavour of the Tsarina Catherine. One of the chancellor's depressions lasted for an unusually long period of time. Serious maladministration was the result; files piled up in the registries, which the Tsarina demanded must be dealt with – but this was impossible without Potemkin's signature. The high officials did not know what to do.

At this time, it just so happened that an insignificant little clerk called Schuvalkin turned up in the antechamber of the chancellor's palace, where the privy councillors were wailing and lamenting as usual. 'What is the matter, my excellencies? How might I be of service to my excellencies?' enquired the zealous Schuvalkin. The situation was explained to him and it was regretted that his services could not be put to any use. 'If it is nothing more than that, gentlemen', answered Schuvalkin, 'then leave the files with me. I kindly ask you.' The state councillors, who had nothing to lose, let themselves be persuaded, and Schuvalkin made his way, with the bundle of papers under his arm, through galleries and corridors, to Potemkin's bedroom. Without knocking, without even halting, he pushed down the door handle. The room was not locked.

In the semi-darkness Potemkin was sitting on his bed, chewing his nails, in a threadbare dressing gown. Schuvalkin stepped up to the desk, dipped the quill in ink, and without saying a word, thrust it into Potemkin's hand, with the first available file on his knee. With an absent glance at the intruder, as though in sleep, Potemkin administered the signature; then a second one, until all were done. When the last one was secured, Schuvalkin left the chamber without a fuss, just as he had entered, with his dossier under his arm. Triumphantly waving the files, Schuvalkin entered the antechamber. The privy councillors fell on him, ripping the papers from his hands. Breathlessly they bent over them. No one said a word; the group froze. Once again, the clerk approached them, once again he enquired hastily as to the cause of the gentlemen's dismay. At that moment his gaze fell on the signature. One file after another was signed: Schuvalkin, Schuvalkin, Schuvalkin ...

The Wish

In a Hasidic village, on the evening of the Sabbath's end, the Jews were sitting at a humble inn. They were all locals, except for one, whom nobody knew: a very poor man, dressed in rags, who cowered in the background in the shadow of the stove. The conversations had gone back and forth. Then one of them brought up the question of what each of them would wish, if he were given one wish. One wanted money, another a son-in-law, and the third a new carpenter's bench, and so they went around.

Once everyone had had their say, there remained only the beggar in the corner by the stove. Reluctantly and hesitantly he gave in to the question: 'I wish I would be an all-powerful king who ruled over a vast land, and at night I would lie asleep in my castle and the enemy would break in past the border and, before dawn, horsemen would reach my castle, meet with no resistance, and, woken in alarm from my sleep, I would not even have time to dress myself, and, wearing only a shirt, I would escape past mountains and valleys and past forests and hills without respite day and night, until I arrived safely here at this bench in your corner. That is what I would wish for.'

The rest of them looked at each other uncomprehendingly. 'And what would come from all that?' asked one. 'A shirt' was the answer.

Thanks

Beppo Aquistapace was employed at a New York bank. The modest man lived only for his work. In four years of service he had been absent at most three times and never without a good excuse. It was all the more noticeable therefore when one day he unexpectedly did not turn up. When on the next day, too, neither the man nor his excuse arrived, Mr McCormik, the staff manager, began to ask around in Aquistapace's office. But nobody could give him any information. The missing fellow entertained few relations with his colleagues; he kept company with Italians, who, like him, came from humble backgrounds. He referred to just this matter in a communication which provided Mr McCormik with information about his whereabouts a week later.

This letter came from the remand prison. In it, Aquistapace appealed to his manager with words that were as composed as they were urgent. A regrettable incident at his local bar, in which he was completely uninvolved, had led to his arrest. To this day he was unable to specify what caused the knife fight between his compatriots. Unfortunately it had claimed a casualty. He knew no one besides Mr McCormik who could vouch for his good name. McCormik, in turn, not only had a certain interest in the dutiful work of the arrested man, he also had connections which made it easy for him to put in a word for Aquistapace with the relevant authorities. Aquistapace had been incarcerated for only ten days when he resumed his duties at the bank. After the office had closed he called on Mr McCormik. Timidly he stood in front of his boss. 'Mr McCormik', he began, 'I don't know how to thank you. Only to you do I owe my release. Believe me, nothing would give me greater pleasure than to show you my gratitude. Unfortunately, I am a poor man. And', he added with a modest smile, 'as you well know, I do not earn a fortune in the bank. But Mr McCormik', he concluded with a firm voice, 'I can assure you of one thing: if ever you should be in a situation whereby elimination of a third person could be profitable, then just remember me. You can count on me.'

—

Translated by Sam Dolbear and Esther Leslie.

The 'Four Tales' have appeared in various versions. One version of 'The Warning' appeared under the title 'Chinoiserie' in *Köl-nische Zeitung*, 22 July 1933; another version appeared in the *Basler Nachrichten*, 26 September 1935. 'The Signature' and 'Thanks' appeared in the *Frankfurter Zeitung*, 5 September 1934, under the pseudonym Detlef Holz. A Danish version of 'The Signature' appeared in *Politiken Magasiner*, Copenhagen, 16 September 1934. The stories were published as a group in the *Prager Tageblatt*, 5 August 1934. The versions here follow an unpublished typescript with handwritten corrections. 'The Signature' finds a similar form at the beginning of Benjamin's 1934 essay on Franz Kafka, and 'The Wish' appears in the same essay in the section titled 'Sancho Pansa'. *Gesammelte Schriften IV*, 757–61.

Opening chapter image: *The Virtue Wagon (to the Memory of October 5, 1922) (Die Tugen Wagon [zur Erinnerung an 5. Oktober 1922])*, 1922.

CHAPTER 39

On the Minute

After an application process lasting months, I finally got a commission from the station management at D to entertain the listeners for twenty minutes with a report from my specialist area, booklore. Were it to be the case that my chatting found an echo, then there was the prospect of a regular repetition of such dispatches. The department manager was kind enough to point out to me that crucial, alongside the composition of such reflections, is the manner of their delivery. 'Beginners', he said, 'commit the error of believing that they are holding their lecture in front of a greater or lesser public, which just happens to be invisible. Nothing could be further from the truth. The radio listener is almost always alone. And even assuming that one reaches thousands of listeners, one is only ever reaching thousands of single listeners. One should always act as if one is speaking to a single person – or to lots of single people, if you wish – but never to many gathered together. That is one thing. And now another thing: stick exactly to the time. If you don't do it, then we have to do it in your place, namely by ruthlessly pulling the plug. Every delay, even the smallest one has, as we know from experience, the tendency to multiply itself in the course of the programme schedule. If we don't intervene instantly, the programming goes off the rails. So don't forget – informal style of presentation! And finish on the dot!'

I followed these instructions very closely: a lot was at stake for me with the recording of my first programme. The manuscript, with which I presented myself at the radio station at the appointed hour, had been read out loud at home against the clock. The announcer received me courteously, and I took it as a special sign of trust that he abstained from monitoring my debut from an adjoining booth. Between the introduction and the sign off, I was my own boss. For the first time ever, I was standing in a modern broadcast studio, where everything was set up to serve the complete comfort of the speaker, the uninhibited blossoming of his abilities. He may stand at a lectern or sit down in one of the commodious armchairs. He has a choice between various sources of light. He can even walk up and down taking the microphone with him. And finally a long case clock whose face marks only minutes, not hours, ensures he is aware of how much the moment is worth in this sealed chamber. When the pointer points to forty, I must be finished.

I had read at least half of my manuscript when I turned

to look at the standing clock, on which the second hand was taking the same circuit as the minute hand, but at sixty times the speed. Had I committed an error at home in my self-direction? Had I made a mistake in my pacing? One thing was clear, two-thirds of my speaking time had passed. As I read on further, word for word, with an engaging tone of voice, I sought feverishly in silence for a way out. Only decisive action would help: whole sections needed to be sacrificed. The considerations leading up to the conclusion would have to be improvised. Tearing myself away from my text was not without its dangers. But I had no other choice. I mustered my energy, turned over several pages of my manuscript, while I dwelled for an extended period, and finally landed happily, like a pilot on his airfield, into the sphere of thought of the concluding section. Breathing again, I immediately gathered together my papers and in the elation of the par force achievement, which I had pulled off, I stepped away from the lectern in order calmly to put on my overcoat.

At this point the announcer should have entered. But he was a long time coming, so I turned towards the door. In so doing, my eye fell again on the long case clock. Its minute hand showed thirty-six! – a whole four minutes until forty. What I had registered earlier on the fly must have been the position of the *second hand*! Now I understood why the announcer was missing. But at the same moment the silence, which had just now been pleasant, surrounded me like a net. In this chamber dedicated to technology and the humans that rule through it, a new terror came over me, which was related to the oldest one that we already know. I lent myself an ear, which now suddenly resonated with nothing but its own silence. But I recognised it as that of death, which now ripped through me in a thousand ears and a thousand parlours.

An indescribable terror came over me and, immediately following that, a wild determination. Salvage what can be salvaged, I said to myself, and ripped the manuscript from out of my coat pocket, took the first best sheet from the omitted ones, and began to read with a voice which seemed to drown out my heartbeat. I was lost for any other ideas. And since the piece of text which I had grabbed was short, I stretched the syllables, let the vowels soar up, rolled the *R*s and inserted meaningful pauses between sentences. Once again, in this manner, I reached the end – the correct one this time. The announcer came and released me, obligingly, just as he had greeted me earlier. But my disquiet persisted. Therefore when, the next day, I met a friend, whom I knew had heard me, I asked casually for his impression. 'It was very nice', he said, 'only the radio receivers have a weakness. My one had a whole minute's interruption again.'

—

Translated by Esther Leslie.

First published in *Frankfurter Zeitung*, 6 December 1934 under the pseudonym Detlef Holz; *Gesammelte Schriften IV*, 761–3; also translated in Walter Benjamin, *'The Work of Art in the Age of Its Technological Reproducibility' and Other Writings on Media*, 407–9.

Opening chapter image: *Christ Child with Yellow Wings (Christkind ohne Flügel)*, 1883.

CHAPTER 40

The Lucky Hand
A Conversation about Gambling

'One simply has to have a lucky hand', said the Dane. 'I could tell you a story ...'

'No story!' interjected the host. 'I want to know your own opinion: do you believe that everything comes down to chance in gambling, or is something else involved?'

There were four of us. My old friend Fritjof, the novelist; the Danish sculptor, to whom he had introduced me in Nice; the shrewd and well-travelled hotelier, on whose terrace we were drinking our afternoon tea; and me. I can't remember anymore how the conversation got around to gambling. I myself had barely joined in, but rather had been devoting myself to the spring sunshine and the feeling of contentment which came from having met my Nice friends here in remote Saint Paul.

With every day that passed, I understood better why Fritjof had chosen this corner to recommence the work on his novel, which he had been unable to make any progress with in Nice. At any rate, that was what I had concluded from the fact that some weeks ago, in response to a question about it, he had answered with an indefinable smile, 'I have lost my fountain pen'. Soon afterwards, I departed and so my joy in seeing Fritjof and his Danish friend here again was all the greater. Of course it was not without some surprise. Had Fritjof, the poor devil, for once actually managed to get a room in a pleasant hotel?

Now we were sitting here in cosy seclusion from the world and, while we chatted, we let our glances rest on the semaphore that waved from a washing line over the city gate or from staggered trees in the valley.

'If you want to hear what I think', said the Dane, 'then it doesn't really depend on any of the things that we have discussed up until now. Neither on the gambling budget, nor on the so-called system, nor on the temperament of the gambler. Indeed it has to do rather with his lack of temperament.'

'I really don't get what you mean.'

'If you had seen with your own eyes what I saw take place in San Remo last month, you would understand right away.'

'Well?' I responded, now curious.

'I arrived', the Dane explained, 'at a casino late in the evening and went up to a table where a game of baccarat had just begun. One seat was still free. It was reserved, and the glances that occasionally fell on it revealed that someone was expected. I was on the point of asking about this guest, who appeared to arouse such anticipation, when I heard someone close by mention the name and, in the same moment, the Marchesina Dal Pozzo herself approached the table, flanked by an usher on one side and her secretary on the other. The journey from the vehicle to her seat seemed to have taken it out of the old lady. Barely had she reached it than she collapsed. After a while, when the dealing shoe reached her and it was her turn to hold the bank, she opened her bag, in no great hurry, and brought out a small pack of hounds in porcelain, glass and jade, her mascots, which she distributed around her seat. She took her time to do this too and then she plunged her hand once more into the depths of her bag and pulled out a bundle of thousand-lira notes. She left the bother of counting them to the croupier. She dealt the cards, but barely had she distributed the last one when she collapsed once again. She didn't even hear the request for another one, with which her partner wished to improve his game. For she was asleep. Now it was possible to see how her secretary rendered outstanding services for her and, respectfully, with a gentle hand, which one could see was well practiced, woke her. Deliberately, the Marchesina disclosed her points, one after the other. "Neuf à la banque", said the croupier; she had won. But that only seemed to send her to sleep. And however many thousand-lira notes she won from this bank, barely a single time passed without the secretary having to prompt her to her good fortune.'

'God looks after his own in sleep,' I said.

'Or should one not rather say in this case, "The Devil looks after his own"?' said the hotelier with a smile.

'Do you know', Fritjof said instead of giving a response, 'that I have sometimes posed myself the question of why gambling is something to be condemned. Of course there is nothing puzzling about it. There are plenty of suicides, frauds and the rest occasioned by gambling. But, as said, is that all?'

'There is something unnatural about gambling,' said the Dane.

'In my opinion', I said, 'it seems all too natural. As natural as the inexhaustible, never depleted hope that we will be lucky.'

'So you give me', responded the Dane, 'the motto "Faith, love, hope". And now look at what has become of it!'

'You mean that your object is unworthy of it. "Filthy lucre!" or suchlike – if I understand you correctly.'

'But he does not understand me correctly,' said the Dane, suddenly turning away from me and towards Fritjof. 'Have you', he continued, looking penetratingly at him, 'ever found yourself on a train or on a bench in the park in direct proximity to a woman who struck you as charming? But really right close up to her?'

'Let me say something to you', replied Fritjof. 'If she is really sitting so close to you, then you will be barely able to see her clearly. Why? Because at such extreme closeness, it is nigh on impossible to behold her. To me, at least, that would seem an impertinence.'

'Then you will understand me all the better, if I now return to our question. We spoke of hope and I compared hope to a young and pretty stranger. It would be impudent to eye her from all too great a nearness or even to approach her with a glance.'

'How come?' I asked, for I was on the point of losing the thread.

'I spoke of temporal closeness,' said the Dane. 'It is my belief that it makes a huge difference whether I cherish a wish directed to a distant future or at the instant. "What one wishes for in one's youth, one has in abundance in old age," says Goethe. The earlier in life one makes a wish, the greater the prospects that it will be fulfilled … but I have gone off-topic.'

'I presume that you wanted to say', Fritjof remarked, 'that someone who gambles also makes a wish.'

'Yes, but one that the very next moment must grant. And that is what is so depraved about it.'

'This is a weird context in which to place gambling', said the hotelier. 'And the opposite to the ivory ball rolling into its pocket would be the shooting star which dives in the distance and grants a wish in that way.'

'Yes, the right wish, which is oriented to the future', said the Dane.

There was a pause after these words. But for me they had cast new light on the old phrase 'unlucky at cards, lucky in love'. As if he wanted to delve into my musings, I heard Fritjof say pensively: 'This much is sure – there are more charms to gambling than winning. Aren't some people looking for a scuffle with fate? Or the opportunity to court it? Believe me: lots of scores are settled on the green cloth – outsiders to the game have no idea of this.'

'It must really be very tempting to test out one's compliance with fate.'

'You never know how it will turn out,' said the hotelier. 'I remember a scene that I witnessed in Montevideo. I lived there for quite a long time when I was a young man. The largest casino in Uruguay is there: people travel for eight hours from Buenos Aires to spend their weekends gambling there. One evening, I was in the casino, just watching. To be on the safe side, I didn't take any money with me. Two young people were standing in front of me, playing intently. They put down small bets, but lots of them. However, they had no luck at all. And soon one of them had lost everything. The other one had a few chips still, which he no longer wanted to bet with. So they interrupted their play, but remained standing there in order to watch that of the others. They were silent and humble for a long time, as losers often are, when suddenly one of them, the one with nothing left, became lively again. He whispered to his friend: "thirty-four!" His friend was simply content to shrug his shoulders. But indeed thirty-four came up. The scryer, who was of course in some distress, tried again. "Seven or twenty-eight!" he murmured to his neighbour, who smiled impassively. And the even number indeed came up. Now the first lad was getting very agitated. Almost imploringly, he whispered "twenty-two". He repeated it three times, in vain: when the twenty-two came up, its pocket was unoccupied. An altercation between the two friends appeared inevitable. But just as the miracle man, shaking with excitement, was about to turn to his neighbour again,the friend, no longer wishing to stand in the way of their common luck, handed him the money. He placed it on the number four. Fifteen came up. He occupied twenty-seven. Zero came up. And he placed and lost the last two chips in a single go. Defeated and reconciled, the two fled the scene.'

'Remarkable!' said Fritjof. 'One might have thought that holding the chips in his hand had suddenly taken from him his gift of seeing into the future.'

'One could just as well say', said the Dane, 'that his gift for seeing into the future robbed him of his winnings.'

'That is an empty paradox', I interjected.

'Not at all', the answer came back. 'If there really is such a thing as a lucky gambler, that is, a telepathic mechanism in gambling, then it resides in the unconscious. It is unconscious knowledge that, if played successfully, translates itself into movements. If on the other hand it migrates to the consciousness, then it is lost for innervation. Our man will "think" the correct thing but he will "act" wrongly. He will stand there like so many other losers who tear their hair out and cry "I knew it!"'

'So, according to you, a lucky gambler operates according to instinct? Like any person at a moment of danger?'

'The game', the Dane confirmed, 'is really an artificially induced danger. And gambling is effectively a blasphemous test of our presence of mind. For in danger the body makes an accord with things that goes over and above our heads. Only once we breathe a sigh of relief, upon being saved, do we think about what we have been through. In acting we are ahead of our knowledge. And gambling is a disreputable affair because it unscrupulously provokes all the finest and most precise things that our organism affords.'

There was a silence. 'One simply has to have a lucky hand' was running through my head. Didn't the Dane want to tell us something about that earlier? I reminded him of this fact.

'Ah, the story', he said smilingly. 'Actually it is a bit late for that – incidentally we know its hero. And we all like him very much. I will simply reveal that he is a writer. That plays a role, you see, although – but I am just about to ruin the punchline. In a word, the man was determined to seek his fortune on the Riviera. He had no idea about gambling, tried this and that system and lost with all of them. Then he gave his systems up and stuck only with losing. His cash resources were soon all used up, his nerves even more so, and then, one day, he even lost his fountain pen. Writers are, as you know, sometimes odd, and our friend belongs to the oddest. He has to have a very particular lighting around his writing desk and a very particular type of paper and a very specific shape and size of his sheets, or else he cannot work. Therefore you can easily imagine what a lost fountain pen would mean to him. After we had frittered away a whole day searching in vain for a new one, we dropped in at the casino in the evening. I never play and contented myself with following our friend's gambling. Soon it was not just me following it. This man was attracting the attention of lots of casino visitors, for he was winning non-stop. After a jolly hour, we left in order to take our cash somewhere secure, at least for this one night. But the next day couldn't harm it. For, as hopeless as the morning in the stationery shops had been, the more lucrative did the evening make itself. Of course there was no longer any talk of the novel, since the fountain pen had disappeared. Our friend, otherwise an industrious man, didn't even look at his manuscript, indeed even avoided the shortest letter. If I reminded him of some especially urgent piece of correspondence, he made excuses. He became parsimonious with his handshakes. He avoided carrying even the lightest little package. He barely turned the pages of his book while reading. It was as if his hand was resting in a bandage, which was taken off only in the evening – in the casino, where we never stayed for very long. We had amassed a tidy sum, when one day the porter at the hotel brought us the fountain pen. It had been found in the palm garden. Our friend gave the bearer a handsome tip, and he departed on the same day, in order to finally write his novel.'

'Lovely', said the hotelier, 'but what does it prove?'

I did not care what the story proved or disproved, and I was glad to see my old friend Fritjof, on whom life had seldom smiled, drink his afternoon tea so sanguinely on the walls of Saint Paul.

—

Translated by Esther Leslie.

Written 1935; unpublished in Benjamin's lifetime. Manuscript bears the pseudonym Detlef Holz. *Gesammelte Schriften IV*, 771–7.

Opening chapter image: *Christ Child Without Wings (Christkind mit gelben Flüglen)*, 1885.

CHAPTER 41

Colonial Pedagogy: Review of Alois Jalkotzy, The Fairy Tale and the Present

Alois Jalkotzy, The Fairy Tale and the Present: The German Folk Tale and Our Time, *Vienna, Jungbrunnen, 1930*

There is something peculiar about this book: the fact is the cover gives it away right from the start. It is a photomontage: winding towers, skyscrapers, factory chimneys in the background, a powerful locomotive in the middle distance and, at the front of this landscape of concrete, asphalt and steel, a dozen children gathered around their nursery teacher, who is telling a fairy tale. It is incontestable that whoever engages with the measures which the author recommends in the text will convey just as much of the fairy tale as the person who relates it at the foot of a steam hammer or inside a boilermaker. And the children will have just as much in their hearts of the reformed fairy tales that are earmarked for them here as their lungs have of the cement desert into which this admirable spokesman 'of our present' relocates them. It is not easy to find a book which demands the relinquishment of that which is most genuine and original with the same taken-for-grantedness that unreservedly dismisses a child's delicate and hermetic fantasy as an emotional demand, having understood it from the perspective of a commodity-producing society, in which education is regarded with such dismal impartiality as an opportunity for colonial sales of cultural wares. The type of child psychology in which the author is well versed is the exact counterpart to that famous 'psychology of primitive peoples' as heaven-sent consumers of European junk wares. It exposes itself from all sides: '*The fairy tale allows the child to equate itself with the hero*. This need for identification corresponds to the infantile weakness, which it experiences in relation to the adult world.' To appeal to Freud's fantastic interpretation of infantile superiority (in his study on narcissism), or even to experience itself, which confirms just the opposite, would be to take too much trouble with a text in which superficiality is proclaimed so fanatically, unleashing, under the banner of the contemporary moment, a holy war against everything that does not correspond to the 'present sensibility' and which places children (like certain African tribes) in the first line of battle.

'The elements from which the fairy tale draws are frequently unusable, antiquated and alien to our contemporary sensibilities. A special role is played by the evil stepmother. Child murderers and cannibals are typical figures of the German folk and fairy tale. The thirst for blood is striking, the portrayal of murder and killing is favoured. Even the supernatural world of the fairy tale is, above all, frightening. Grimms' collection teems with the lust for beatings. The German folk and fairy tale is frequently pro-alcohol, or at least never opposed to alcohol.' And so the times move on. While, to conclude along the lines of the author, the cannibal must have been a rather common feature of German everyday life until quite recently, he is now somewhat alienated from 'contemporary sensibilities'. That may be so. But what if children, given the choice, would rather run into his throat than into that of the new pedagogy? And thereby for their part prove themselves likewise to be alienated from the 'contemporary sensibility'? Then it will be hard to captivate them again with the radio, 'this miracle of technology', from which the author expects a new blossoming of the fairy tale. For 'the fairy tale necessitates … narration as the most important expression of life'. This is what the language of a man who approaches the work of the Grimm Brothers in order to adapt it to particular 'needs' looks like. Because he shies away from nothing, he even provides samples of such adaptation in a procedure that substitutes the spinning wheel by the sewing machine, and royal castles by stately homes. For 'the monarchical polish of our Central European world is happily overcome, and the less we place this spook and nightmare of German history in front of our children, the better will it be for our children and for the development of the German nation and its democracy'. No! The night of our republic is not so dark that all the cats in it are grey and Wilhelm II and King

Thrushbeard can no longer be distinguished from each other. It will still find the energy to block the path of this fun-loving reformism, for which psychology, folklore and pedagogy are only flags under which the fairy tale as an export commodity is freighted to a dark corner of the globe, where the children in the plantations yearn for its pious mode of thinking.

—

Translated by Esther Leslie.

First published in *Frankfurter Zeitung*, 21 December 1930; *Gesammelte Schriften III*, 272–4.

Opening chapter image: *Ugly Angel (Hässlicher Engel)*, 1939.

CHAPTER 42

Verdant Elements: Review of
Tom Seidemann-Freud,
Play Primer 2 *and* 3
Something More on the Play Primer

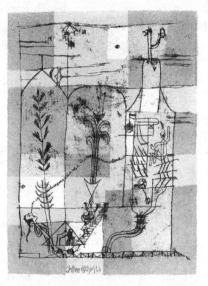

Tom Seidmann-Freud, Spielfibel 2 *and* Hurra, wir rechnen!
Spielfibel 3, *Berlin: Herbert Stuffer Verlag, 1931*

One year ago (13 December 1930) the *Frankfurter Zeitung* introduced its readers to the first play primer by Tom Seidmann-Freud. The idea back then was to loosen up the primer in a playful way, represent its historical development and, at the same time, give some indication of the circumstances which act as preconditions for this most recent and most radical solution. In the meantime, the enterprise has advanced further: the second part of the reading primer and the first part of the arithmetic primer are now available. Yet again, the two methodological guiding themes have been retained most brilliantly: the complete activation of the drive to play through the most intimate association of writing and drawing, and the affirmation of infantile self-confidence by the expansion of the primer into an encyclopaedia. This provides us with an opportunity to recall one of the crucial sentences from the introduction to the first play primer: 'It is not oriented towards "appropriation" and "mastery" of a particular task – this style of learning only suits grown-ups – rather it takes account of the child, for whom learning, as with everything else, naturally signifies a great adventure.' If, at the beginning of this adventurous journey, flowers and colours, children's names and names of countries were the little islands in the sea of fantasy, then it is now segmented continents, the world of leaves on trees and fish, shops and butterflies, which rise up from the water. Resting places and little huts to lodge in have been provided everywhere: this means that it is not necessary for the child to write on and on to the point of exhaustion. Rather, *there* an image awaits his signature, *here* a story awaits the missing words; *there* again a cage waits for a bird to be sketched in, or – elsewhere – a dog, a donkey and a cock await their woof, bray and cook-a-doodle-do. Groupings and classifications join in, now and again they are even of a lexical type, whereby painted things are written out according to initials, or, just as in a real encyclopaedia, in topics organised by concepts. Small boxes are as good for ABCs as for things made of leather, wood, metal and glass, or for furniture, fruits and objects of everyday use. With all of this, the child is never placed in front of, but rather above the object of instruction: as if, for example, in a zoological class, he or she were not led in front of the horse, but rather placed upon it as a rider. Here every letter, every word and drawing is such a horse, which accompanies all the stages of this learning process. With its curves, just as with its bridle and collar, it is able to bring all that is recalcitrant under the control of the little rider. It is quite extraordinary how, from the beginning, the author also accentuates the power of command, so crucial for childish play, in relation to numbers. The point-system is retired after only a few pages; there follow red or black battalions of fish or insects, butterflies or squirrels – and, if at the end of each sequence, the child sets down a number, then he does not draw the digit any differently than when he plants a sergeant in front of his squad.

At every point the author made sure to guarantee the sovereignty of the player, allowing him never to relinquish any power to the object of learning and banishing the horror with which the first numbers and letters so readily configure themselves as idols before the child. This is surely the way that the older generation recalls the impression – so hard to describe – made on them by the first 'applied tasks' in their arithmetic textbooks. What coldness was spread by the phoney moral uprightness of these lines, into which – like a trap door – numerals were embedded every now and again. It was nothing less than a betrayal by the most trusted and beloved thing that the child had received from his mother: the story. And, therefore, it is a whole world of reconciliation which rings forth from the simple imperative of this maths primer: '8 − 6 = 2. Invent a story to go along with this and write it here.' Part of the charm of these textbooks – and simultaneously their highly pedagogical achievement – is the manner in which they capture the easing of tension that corresponds to their confident attitude, an attitude which the child may, at first, seek outside of these pages. For if, in turn, the child is prepared to natter away about what he has just learnt, to get up to mischief and silliness with it, then this book is, once again, his best friend. After all, it contains enough white spots to be painted and scribbled on, broad fertile territories on which all its owner's monsters and favourites can be settled comfortably. Of course none of this occurs without some clearance work:

> In this story, cross out the following:
> All *A*s and *a*s in red
> All *R*s and *r*s in blue
> All *D*s and *d*s in green
> All *L*s and *l*s in brown.

But, oh, the parties to which one gets invited after the work is done! Garlands, which had already cropped up in the first primer as traces of the 'writing tower', wind their way through the land of reading and the letters assume carnivalesque disguises. 'Onca ipon e tuma thara wes a luttla gurl, who hed e meguc cet. Thus cet coild spaak': so it begins in a dialect between old high German and thieves' slang. In addition, however, there is sufficient room for an unmasking: 'Copy down the story, but replace every *a* with an *e* and vice versa; for every *i* put a *u* and vice versa.' Quite underhandedly an old pedagogical bone of contention is thus resolved: whether, when it comes to children, one may model error as a warning. The answer: yes, as long as one exaggerates. Hence it is exaggeration, the experienced confidante of the littlest ones, which protectively places its hand over so many pages of this primer.

Or is it a case of not exaggerating a lie when a story begins as follows? 'A boy with the name Eve got up one morning from the closet and sat down to eat his evening meal.' Is it any surprise if such a person concludes his day by plucking chocolate biscuits, which grow in the grass, until he gets hungry? It is certain that the child feasts itself on such stories. Another story begins: Adolf lived at the house of a bumpkin together with little Cecily – is that not an exaggeration of the world order, to allow all the nouns up to 'witchcraft' and 'Yucatan' to appear in the story in the correct alphabetic sequence? In the end, does it not mean exaggerating even the regard for the preschool pupil? To place questionnaires in front of him as before a professor: what are you doing on Monday? Tuesday? Wednesday? etc., or to cover a table for him with lined plates on which he may write his favourite meals? – Yes. But Shock-Headed Peter, too, is exaggerated, Max and Moritz are exaggerated, as is Gulliver. Robinson's loneliness is exaggerated and so is what Alice saw in Wonderland – why should not letters and numbers also have to authenticate themselves in front of children through their exaggerated exuberance? Certainly their challenges will still be strict enough.

Perhaps some person or another (such as the writer of these lines) has held onto the primer from which his mother learnt to read. 'Egg', 'whee', 'mouse' – its first pages may have begun this way. I won't say a word against this primer. How could anything negative be said by he who learnt from it how to rebel against it? Of all the things that he encountered later in life, what could rival the rigour and certainty with which he approached these strokes; what subsequent submission filled him with such a strong sense of immeasurable import as the surrender to the letter? Nothing against this old primer then. But it was 'the seriousness of life' which spoke therefrom, and

the finger that followed along its lines had crossed the threshold of a realm from which no wanderer returns: he was under
the spell of the black-upon-white, of law and right, the irrevo-
cable, the being set for all eternity. We know today what we
should think of such things. Perhaps the misery, lawlessness
and insecurity of our days is the price for which we alone can
pursue the enchanting-debunking game with type, from which
these primers by Seidmann-Freud acquire such deep reason.

—

Translated by Esther Leslie.

Written 1931; published in *Frankfurter Zeitung*, 20 December
1931; *Gesammelte Schriften III*, 311–14.

Opening chapter image: *Hoffmanesque Scene (Hoffmanneske
Szene)*, 1921.

Translators' Note

The texts were translated by Sam Dolbear, Esther Leslie and Sebastian Truskolaski, except for 'Nordic Sea', which was jointly translated by Sam Dolbear and Antonia Grousdanidou. Although the editors checked one another's drafts, each text acknowledges its principal translator. Thanks to Ursula Marx at the Walter Benjamin Archiv. In addition, Sam Dolbear would like to thank the following people for their invaluable assistance in preparing and refining the drafts: Koshka Duff, Miriam Gartner, Robin Kreutel, Magda Schmukalla, and Cat Moir. On the whole, as editors, we concentrated on previously untranslated work, but included a handful of previously translated pieces for the sake of internal consistency.

About the Illustrations
Paul Klee

A Klee drawing named 'Angelus Novus' shows an angel looking as though he is about to move away from something he is fixedly contemplating. His eyes are staring, his mouth is open, his wings are spread. This is how one pictures the Angel of History. His face is turned toward the past. Where we perceive a chain of events, he sees one single catastrophe that keeps piling ruin upon ruin and hurls it in front of his feet. The angel would like to stay, awaken the dead, and make whole what has been smashed. But a storm is blowing from Paradise; it has got caught in his wings with such violence that the angel can no longer close them. The storm irresistibly propels him into the future to which his back is turned, while the pile of debris before him grows skyward. This storm is what we call progress.

– Walter Benjamin, Thesis IX, 'On the Concept of History'

In 1921, Walter Benjamin purchased Paul Klee's *Angelus Novus*, the drawing that opens this book, which became one of his most prized possessions. Remarkable for their simplicity, humor and fantastical nature, Klee's illustrations here bring to life Benjamin's stories.

PAUL KLEE (1879–1940) was a Swiss-German painter and an important figure in the development of modern art, known for his explorations in color and line in his work. His extensive writing on color theory and lectures while a teacher at the Bauhaus from 1921 to 1931 were collected as *Writings on Form and Design Theory* (*Schriften zur Form und Gestaltungslehre*), published in English as the *Paul Klee Notebooks*, and are considered a foundational text in the understanding of modern art. In 1937, more than a hundred of Klee's works were labeled as 'degenerate art' and seized from public collections in Germany by the Nazis.

Opening image: *Self Portrait*, 1911.